Savannah's Star

Savannah's Star

SHOOTING STAR SERIES BOOK 2

LESLEY ESPOSITO

authorHOUSE®

AuthorHouse™ LLC
1663 Liberty Drive
Bloomington, IN 47403
www.authorhouse.com
Phone: 1-800-839-8640

Published by AuthorHouse   07/05/2013

ISBN: 978-1-4817-6803-0 (sc)
ISBN: 978-1-4817-6804-7 (e)

Library of Congress Control Number: 2013911491

To Sharon and Charles
And an amazing life
Full of adventure

Chapter 1

Molly and Katie had left the city for another girl's weekend. Since Molly graduated college with her Masters in Education this was their third trip together. They had gone to Washington D.C. and Nantucket Island. This time they were spending a long weekend at the beach in Virginia. So far all of their trips had been long weekends. They both had limited time off due to their jobs and limited time in general since Molly's wedding was coming up and she was in the middle of an apartment renovation. Best friends since middle school, they were inseparable. Despite them working opposite hours they made a point to get away, girls only.

This trip was a little more special as it would be Molly's last time going as a single woman. Katie had wanted to go some place more exotic but, due to time constraints, they opted to go where they could drive. Well, where Katie was willing to drive anyway, as Molly still did not have a driver's license. They also compromised on the amount of night life. Katie would have been happy in Atlantic City with casinos and nightlife. Molly absolutely refused. Not only would she never gamble any of her money, she had no need for loud and crazy nightlife. They eventually agreed on an upscale hotel with restaurants and bars. Katie was still single so Molly had to give in somewhat.

If Molly had to go out to the bar at night then Katie had to go on a kayaking trip with Molly. She would have been content to stay on the beach all day but it was her best friend's weekend so she agreed. She felt ridiculous in the oversized life vest sitting in the tiny boat on the sand. It was early in the morning and it was already hot. She had to keep swatting at the mosquitoes and sweat was already running down her back. The guide, Emma, was giving a lesson on paddling and steering but Katie was not paying much attention. This was not her idea of fun. She looked at Molly and gave her a lopsided grin and thumbs up saying "I better not fall out of this thing."

"Well if you pay attention you might learn how not to," Molly said back. She was paying close attention. She had no intention of falling out either. She was determined to try something new with every trip she took whether it was food, a museum or an adventure. This definitely was an adventure. She wished Jason, her fiancé, was there with her though. He would make sure nothing happened but it was good for her to try new things on her own as well. She looked back down at the foot pedals that would move the rudder which would allow her to turn. Okay, right pedal to turn right but paddle left, she held the paddle up as she pressed the pedal. She thought one should have a driver's license to operate the kayak but of course she did not. "Would you relax," Katie told her, "you will be fine once we get out on the water."

"Easy for you to say, you already know how to steer a moving vehicle." Molly took a deep breath and put her paddle down. Katie was right though. What could possibly happen?

Emma, the guide, was going down the line of kayaks pushing each one into the water. There were four others in the group and Molly and Katie were the last two to go in the water. When Katie's boat went in the water she let out a little yelp. The boat wobbled in the water then it started spinning in a slow drifting circle.

"I'm drifting and I'm going to fall out," Katie yelled to no one in particular.

"Don't worry, just relax. Make sure you are seated in the center and start paddling back to the group," Emma instructed.

Katie laughed at her friend but when she entered the water and felt the boat settle she understood Katie's concern. The current easily took the boat in its own direction. Molly picked up her paddle, found her foot pedals and started testing her paddling skills. The guide kept the small group together and took them through a series of quick lessons on turning.

Katie and Molly were fairly quick studies but they did manage to scrape boats a few times. Emma assured them it was common and not to worry. The hardest part of the tour was staying out of the way of the motor boats cruising out towards the open waters of the Chesapeake Bay but that was only for a short period as they made their way deeper into the protected areas of the park.

"I would much rather be on one of those boats," Katie said.

"But these kayaks require no gas, just pure human power," Molly replied as she dug her paddle a little harder in the water.

"Exactly my problem," Katie grumbled as she struggled to push through the initial current. When the water smoothed out she relaxed a little as she was able to keep up with the group.

"It's so beautiful here and no motor boat can get in here."

Katie silently conceded the point. She did not want Molly to know how much she was enjoying herself. They finally reached water that was smooth as glass; the trees rooted in the water were haunting with Spanish moss dripping from the branches. They came across great herons, snowy egrets, turtles and ducks.

The group drifted along at a leisurely pace with no set destination. They followed the wildlife or stopped to check out the gnarled shapes of the trees. Emma paddled around the group taking photos.

Molly was glad someone else was taking pictures. She was too scared to take her camera. She figured it would end up in the water. It was the very first gift Jason gave her and she still treasured it. She planned on ordering photos from Emma. She hoped there would be one of Katie smiling. She knew Katie was enjoying the tour mostly because she stopped complaining and was quiet for a change.

The tour ended back at the small beach, they paddled their boats onto the sand. Emma's assistant Alex pulled each one up higher on top of the sand so they would not have to step in the water to get out.

"I definitely like the scenery here," Katie said as she watched Alex flex his muscles. He appeared to be college age, was tan and all around sexy.

"He's too young for you don't you think?"

"No, not for a little weekend fling."

"Whatever," Molly rolled her eyes. Katie was always scoping out the guys.

"Hey, you never know! Your week long fling turned into a marriage," she reminded her.

Molly did not deny that. A chance meeting had led her and her fiancé on a trip that turned into romance. Despite some obstacles they made their way back to each other and were soon to be married.

They all clambered out of their boats and stood together for one last group shot. Emma thanked them for taking her tour and gave them business cards to view their photos.

Katie went to Emma to ask about the local scene. "Where do you go for good drinks and cute guys around here?"

"Well I actually have not lived here for very long but there is a restaurant bar that has excellent crushes down on Third Street. I am often there on Thursday nights."

"Sounds like it could be fun. Maybe we'll see you there."

"Thanks again for coming."

They spent the rest of the afternoon sunning on the beach and swimming in the ocean. The tide was low so the waves were calm. They floated around, hunted for sea shells and watched a pod of dolphins swim by. While they were sitting on the lounge chairs watching a group of surfers walk by Katie asked, "do you think Alex will be at the bar tonight?"

"I have no idea. Find him attractive?"

She shrugged her shoulders in response before laying back. "I was just wondering."

Molly wondered what was so intriguing about him. Katie certainly had her share of dates and boyfriends. While she was pretending not to care too much, Molly could tell she had her eye on him. Of course Molly could not say anything considering how she met Jason.

After dinner and showers they got ready for the night out. They took the trolley the thirty blocks of the oceanfront road. They passed by a variety of hotels big and small. There were restaurants, surf shops, boutiques and the same beach shop appeared every couple of blocks. They took the trolley to the end of the resort strip and were dropped off in front of a two story restaurant facing the oceanfront.

They went inside and went to the second floor to the bigger bar area. There were not too many people just yet so they found a small table overlooking the water and ordered drinks. They chatted about the summer, Molly's wedding and the upcoming school year. Molly was very excited but nervous about teaching her own class for the first time.

When they were on their second round of drinks, Katie noticed Emma and her friends coming in and motioned for them to join her and Molly. They went through the introductions including Emma's roommate

Allie. It turns out that Allie was the assistant manager at the hotel where Molly and Katie were staying.

"I hope you are enjoying your stay."

"So far," Katie answered Allie although she was watching Alex.

Molly jumped in, "the room is beautiful and view is fabulous."

"Glad to hear that. So, what do you do?"

"I just got my Masters in Elementary Education and will be teaching fourth grade in September."

"That's great. Congratulations. How about you Katie?"

It took a moment for Katie to realize she had been asked a question. "Oh, I am a pediatric nurse."

Alex was surprised at that and impressed. He did not like to make judgments about people but Katie did not seem such a serious person. He was definitely intrigued. "A very noble profession but it must be difficult at times."

"Yes, well that is why we let loose on the weekends," she laughed smiling at Molly.

"Yeah, more her than me. So, what do you do other than lugging around kayaks?" Molly asked.

"I am a student," he responded with no other explanation.

Emma gave him a little kick under the table.

"What was that for?" he quietly asked her.

She gave him the look that said why don't you tell them more, but he seldom spoke about himself. He generally stuck with the cute surfer boy attitude while letting few people know how smart he actually was. She sighed and shrugged her shoulders. These ladies were only here for a weekend anyway and they were only just talking.

The night continued on with drinks flowing and good conversation. It was Allie's turn to be the designated driver so she kept to her sweet teas. As the night went on and the noise level picked up the group decided to move outside. They went out on the boardwalk to cool off and take in the night sea air. Alex and Katie broke off from the group and found a spot along the railing for themselves. The other three ladies took a spot on one of the benches and continued with their own conversation. They also noticed the body language between Alex and Katie heating up.

The evening wore on and the three ladies were ready to call it a night. Allie offered to get the car so she could give everyone a ride home. Alex and Katie were not ready to go though.

"I will walk Katie back to the hotel," Alex informed the group.

"Are you sure? It's almost thirty blocks," Emma told them.

"It's fine, right?" he turned to Katie.

Katie readily nodded her head in agreement. She smiled at him but almost in a shy way. Molly rarely saw her like this. She was quieter than usual but in a more sophisticated way. Alex seemed like a good guy so she was fine with them walking back but she definitely would be waiting up for her.

"What do you think?" Molly asked Emma.

"I am good with it. Alex will take care of her."

The group split up. Molly watched Katie walk with Alex for a few minutes before joining Emma to wait for Allie. When Molly caught up with her Emma noticed that she seemed a little restless. It did not take long to find out why.

"Is Katie seeing anyone?" Emma asked.

"No, she's a flirt but only when she is available."

"Has she had a lot of boyfriends in the past?" Emma continued her questioning.

"No, a few were serious but they did not work out."

"Why?"

Molly gave her a slight look of annoyance. She trusted Emma's word on Alex and did not see a need for the twenty questions for a walk.

"I'm sorry; we are just a little protective of Alex. He is Allie's younger brother."

"Well then you will understand when I tell you that Katie has five brothers and she knows who will and will not pass their approval. Besides they are just talking."

"You are right. I'm sorry."

"It's fine. I think it is great. Siblings and friends should watch out for each other. Katie has definitely watched out for me over the years and still does."

"I'm glad you understand." Emma just wished her brother had been a little more interested in who she dated. Perhaps she would not have wasted so many years with her ex if he had. She was living a new life though. Emma turned her attention back to Molly.

"I hope you enjoy the rest of your weekend and have a safe trip back."

"Thanks, I loved your kayak tour and I appreciate the ride back to the hotel."

"No problem. It was a fun night."

Molly was fairly tired by the time she got back to her room and got ready for bed. She turned the television on to help her stay awake while she waited for Katie to return. While she felt she could trust Alex she was still a touch on edge. There was no way she would be able to face Katie's family if anything happened to her. She got up and went out on the balcony. The night air was still warm and there was a breeze blowing off the ocean. She took a deep breath and wished her fiancé was there with her. In just a few weeks they were getting married and she was so excited.

She scanned the boardwalk looking for Katie but she was also mesmerized by the light of the moon dancing on the water. Every so often she would catch a splash on the surface of the water and she wondered if it was another dolphin passing by or perhaps a pelican diving for a midnight snack. Even without the amazing scene she could have stood there content just to listen to the rhythmic breaking of the waves. She caught a shadow across the boardwalk and saw Katie and Alex walking towards the hotel. They looked quite cozy walking hand in hand. They stopped along the rail of the boardwalk and Alex pulled her close to him. Molly felt like she was invading a private moment and she did not want to be caught watching so she went back inside. Content that Katie returned safely, she shut off the television and went to bed.

The next morning Molly quietly went out onto the balcony to watch the sun rise. When she was in St. Lucia a year ago she was able to watch the sunset from the beach so now she wanted to watch the sunrise. She took photographs every few minutes as the sun slowly rose above the horizon. The colors were much more muted than the sunset's intense oranges and pinks. This was more like a pastel palette that gave a slow and gentle wake up call for the new day. When the new light finally became too intense to watch she crept back inside and settled back in bed.

A few hours later the pair decided room service was in order so they could lounge around in their pajamas. When the food arrived they set up on the table by the window. They cracked open the balcony door so they could hear the waves breaking on the shore. The beach was coming alive with families staking their claim on the sand for the day. Kids were building sand castles. Moms were trying to spray sunscreen on the little ones. Others were catching waves or strolling along the water line. Travel had become an important part of Molly's life and someday when she had kids she would take them everywhere as well.

Molly sat down with Katie who was already digging into her breakfast. Molly noticed that she was being unusually quiet this morning. She hoped her evening had ended well. "Did you enjoy your walk?"

"Yes," she said between bites of eggs but gave nothing else away.

Molly picked up a blueberry and threw it at her friend. "Is that all you have to say?"

Katie laughed as she lobbed a raspberry back Molly's way which she managed to catch and pop in her mouth in one swift move. "I don't know if it was the setting but I was definitely attracted to him. He's smart and funny. He's a graduate student. He's studying historical architecture. It was really fascinating."

"Wow that is pretty impressive. Did he tell you he is Allie's brother?"

"Yes, I think it's great they hang out together."

"So, what now?"

"I don't know. He has one more year of school. We'll talk, Skype and see what happens."

Molly knew that her friend was officially off the market even if she was playing it casual. She would support her either way as long as she was happy.

"I'm so glad we got to do this last trip before the wedding. It's getting a little messy around the apartment with all the renovations."

"How is that coming?" Katie asked.

"Slow but good, Ben promised to have it done by the time we get back from Fiji. Isn't it ironic his mother won a trip to the same hotel? He told me about it just before we came. His mother did not want to go so he's coming instead."

"Hmm, interesting. Maybe we should set him up with a certain kayak tour guide?"

Molly laughed. Katie always had dating and matchmaking on her mind. "Maybe I will just suggest the tour and see what happens." The two smiled and toasted to love.

Chapter 2

A week later Ben was pulling into the same hotel. Even though he left work early it was later than he intended. By the time he picked up his rental car the traffic through New Jersey was backing up. Only part of his trip was on actual highways. The other part took him through small and medium sized towns. He felt like every traffic light he came to was red. The only redeeming part of the trip was crossing the Chesapeake Bay Bridge. It was seventeen miles of bridges and tunnels over water and manmade islands. The sun was setting low on the bay making for a spectacular display of colors on the water. He would have stopped to watch more of the sunset but he was running out of steam and he was fairly close to his destination.

The directions to the hotel were straight forward. By the time he got there it was dark so he could not get a good sense of his surroundings. From what he could tell it seemed to be a typical beach resort town with a row of hotels and beach shops. He parked his car and grabbed his one suitcase and carry bag. He was tired and hoped for a speedy check in. He wanted to take a long hot shower then get some sleep.

He entered an open, well-lit lobby. It was clean and nicely decorated. He understood that this was a brand new hotel and was supposed to be one of the nicest in the resort area. He quickly found the guest registration desk and gave his name. The desk clerk excused herself for a moment. Ben became slightly irritated. He was not in the mood for a problem that would cause an argument. He was told there would be no issue changing the name on the reservation.

When the clerk came out she was accompanied by a woman who was well—dressed in business attire. She was tall and blonde with a cheerful demeanor. She was carrying a wrapped gift basket. Of course a beautiful woman could always cheer him up. He gave her one of his irresistible grins.

"Welcome, Ben. My name is Allie Golding and I am the assistant manager at the Blue Dolphin. I want to congratulate you on winning our sweepstakes."

"My mother actually won but she could not be here." He was not going to say that she did not want to be there. She lived near the beach on the west coast and could not see the point in going to an east coast beach. But she would never let something free go to waste so she insisted he go instead. He just hoped it was worth the week he took off from work. So far the view was nice. "I do believe her loss is my gain though."

"Well, we are glad you are here. We have put together a welcome basket for you. It has drinks and snacks, local guides and coupons. Please don't hesitate to ask for anything you need."

"I will keep that in mind."

Allie picked up the envelope with the room keys from the desk. "I will be happy to show you to your room and give you a brief tour."

"After you," he said out of politeness but also so he could check out her backside. Despite being tired he was more than happy to accompany her through the hotel.

Allie nodded and took the lead. She conceded that Ben was good looking with his sandy hair and five o' clock shadow. He was tall and muscular. She could tell he was being polite but definitely in a flirtatious way. It was her job to be cheerful and fully promote the hotel but she had absolutely no interest in dating right now. She pushed on with the tour so she could get him to his room and get back to her office.

As they left the reception area she described the restaurants and bar area. Allie showed him the indoor pool and exercise room before taking the elevator up to the eighth floor. "Do you have anything planned for the week?"

"I'm not sure yet. Probably just hang out and relax." Maybe get to know a few of the locals he thought to himself.

"As part of your prize package you have an umbrella and two chairs reserved in your name on the beach. Will anyone be joining you this week?"

Maybe his charms were starting to work for him and she was feeling him out. "No."

"Well our lounge is very popular with both locals and vacationers if you are interested in meeting people."

Was that an invite? "Maybe I will check it out." After a bad split up he was on a relationship break but that did not rule out dating or a little vacation fun. Maybe someday the right woman would cross his path but this week was more about fun and relaxation.

"Good, here we are. You are at the end of the hall in a suite."

Ben followed his guide down the hall. Allie handed him the key to allow him to open the door. After unlocking the door he gestured for her to enter first. She walked in and placed the basket on the coffee table. Allie continued with her tour guide duties showing him the living room, bedroom and balcony. She pointed out the Jacuzzi tub in the bathroom, Keurig coffee maker and the various electronic amenities. Ben followed her around the two rooms nodding. Finally she made her way to the door.

Allie turned to him. "Do you have any questions?"

"No." He could have asked a bunch of pointless questions but she seemed ready to leave and he did not want to come across as overly interested. He knew when to back off.

"Anything I can get for you this evening."

"No thanks."

"Have a good night then."

"Thank you. Maybe I will see you around?"

Allie gave him her business smile. "I work night shifts so I will be here if you need anything." Allie headed back to her office thinking Ben was nice to look at but typical big ego kind of guy.

Ben closed the door thinking he should be able to think of something he needed from her during the week. For now though a nice shower and some sleep would do him good.

The next morning, Emma and Alex were setting up the kayaks on the beach preparing for their next tour. Some days Alex would join them but today's tour was full so he would meet them back on the beach later on to help load the boats back on the trailer. Emma was the owner, operator and guide for her tour company. She had set up her business early in the spring. She had spent a lot of her own time paddling the various waterways getting to know the area. She learned quickly to gear her tours to the different types of tourists and their different sense of adventure. While she did offer a few options during the summer season most of the people who signed up had never kayaked before and just wanted to experience beautiful scenery without it being too strenuous. That is why she opted to buy the higher end kayaks with rudders that would allow for better steering. Emma limited the number of people per tour so that they would have a more personal experience.

Emma also had a photography business that she incorporated into her tours. She took individual group and nature photographs. She even hand delivered anything ordered to the local hotels. She also had plans to sell her work commercially to local advertising agencies and even to make a book of the local wildlife. She knew there would be fewer tours in the winter so she needed alternative ways to make money.

For now, business was good and this morning was no different than most of the others. The group arrived within minutes of each other. Today there was a family of three, a young couple and a single man. The man was rather attractive Emma noted as she set up the paddles and life vests. She wondered why he was there by himself but the thought quickly passed. She had very little interest in men these days.

"Are we required to wear life vests?" handsome man asked.

"Only those under eighteen are required to wear life vests. The water is calm so it is up to you and your comfort level. If you don't want to wear it just put it under the bungee cords."

Emma turned her attention to the entire group. She introduced herself and went through her routine of explaining the trip and what they would see and encounter. She gave her introduction to paddling speech and then she had the group introduce themselves.

"I am Tom and this is my wife Allison and this is our daughter Christina. We are from Ohio and this is our first time kayaking."

"Are there alligators in this water?" Christina asked with genuine concern. She looked to be about eight and would be paddling with her father.

"No, honey we are too far north for alligators." Emma noted the girl's relief.

"I'm Andy and this is my boyfriend Chris. We live in Danville and we canoe around the lakes by us." Andy had a fairly deep southern accent and the pair seemed to make a cute couple.

"Ben. First time for me too." Ben was on vacation by himself and this tour was specifically recommended to him by one of his clients. He was told the tour was well run with attention to detail. What his client failed to mention was how cute Emma was. Maybe she was playing secret matchmaker but that seemed ridiculous since they lived in different states. In any case, he was there for a week by himself so he was happy to sign up for the tour.

He watched Emma as she pushed the boats in the water and helped the others get situated. She was just above average height with fair skin and light blonde hair that appeared to be naturally highlighted by the sun. But what Ben noticed the most was how incredibly strong she was. Her calves were lean and well defined. Her shoulders were well muscled without being bulky. She was definitely more his type than the hotel manager.

Ben watched her push the boats into the water with ease. Obviously the daily kayaking kept her in great shape. It was his turn and Emma told him how to get in by stepping in the center and sitting down while bringing the other foot in. He let his weight balance the boat while he picked up his paddle. He pushed off and caught up with the rest of the group.

Emma put on her hat, long sleeve sun shirt, put the coolers in her boat and pushed off. She guided the group out of the path of the motor boats. Once they were in an area that was safer she explained they could pretty much make their own course as long as they stayed together. She encouraged them to point out wildlife or any other points of interest they could all check out together. In the meantime she would paddle in and around the group taking photographs.

The group started out with Emma in the lead. They pushed through the moderate current from the launch before heading into the park area where the water was calmer and smoother. Emma turned her boat around and started photographing the group as they drifted by. Ben was at the rear of the group and as he drifted by he turned and smiled at Emma. He put his paddle down and took his shirt off in quite a dramatic fashion stretching his arms high over his head letting Emma get a good look at his well muscled upper body.

Emma lowered her camera and watched the display. While she was impressed with his well-cared for body, she was not impressed with the overt flirtation and she did not return his smile. She did get back in line behind him though basically because she was last in the group. She looked around continuing to shoot nature photos but her eye kept drifting back to Ben. She watched as his muscles contracted with each turn of the paddle. She did admit it would make for an interesting study in motion. She switched her camera setting to black and white and zoomed in on his upper back, shoulders and arms. She also set it on continuous so that the camera would take a series of shots as he paddled on.

When she had enough photos of Ben, Emma put her camera back in its bag. She decided it was time for a little fun. She surged ahead and when she was in the middle of the group again she turned and said, "you all look a little hot." She then dug her paddle deep in the water and flicked water onto Ben and repeated the action on Andy and Chris. Chris then flipped water onto Tom and Christina. Allison tried to get away but her daughter was too quick.

Ben was not going to let Emma be the only dry one in the group. He quietly pulled his boat right behind Emma's and scooped up as much water as his paddle would allow. In one quick, smooth motion he flipped his paddle right alongside Emma and soaked her whole top half. Emma turned with an evil grin and wasted no time in splashing him back. The whole group continued in the water fight until everyone was good and wet. Luckily everyone had a good sense of humor and were enjoying themselves. Emma would only start the water fights if she felt there would be no hurt feelings which she knew meant putting herself in the line of fire as well.

Emma led the group to an area where they could tether together and have a snack break. She passed out waters and offered a variety of small snacks.

Ben had his boat tethered next to Emma's. He did position himself so they would end up side by side. He was very glad he signed up for this trip. Not only was the site-seeing beautiful, he was definitely intrigued with Emma. She was an amazing guide, very knowledgeable of her surroundings and had a great sense of humor. Now that he was cooled off he put his shirt back on. He was a little disappointed that she did not have more of a reaction to his flirting but he was not ready to give up. "Do you ever give private tours?" he asked her.

She responded in a business-like manner. "Not during the summer season. My tours fill up during the tourist season which does not leave a lot of free time."

"Of course, I understand." It made good business sense. He would have to think of another way to see her again this week.

When the snacks were finished Emma collected the trash and they headed off again. They watched as turtles sun bathed, herons fished for food and egrets swooped above their heads. When the tour was over she led the group back to the beach and set her boat back on shore. Alex was waiting on the beach and they both helped pull the boats up on the beach while everyone got out on dry land. Emma took one more group photo, handed out her business card so they could view them online and thanked everyone for coming.

Ben lingered behind for a few minutes. After the rest of the group left he approached Emma. "So how might one see you again?" he asked with his best grin.

"You can sign up for another tour," she responded matter of fact. She was doing her best to ignore direct eye contact with his beautiful blue eyes. She was not interested, Emma kept reminding herself.

"It seems that you are booked up for the rest of the week." When he signed up for this trip a week ago it was, in fact, the only spot available.

"Well, I guess you can keep checking back for cancelations then." She continued to collect the paddles and life vests and started heading up to the van. Emma noticed that he was following her. He obviously was not going to give up too easily. She did not really understand though. She did not know what he saw in her. When Emma turned to close the back door of the van he was standing very close to her. It seems that she had left a vest behind and he brought it with him.

She took it from and thanked him. Ben stood silently watching her. She felt flushed as he studied her face. Emma blushed a little as she felt like a mess. Her shirt was still wet and her hair tangled. It did not seem to bother him though and she ended up studying his face a little longer than intended. She finally let herself admit that he was good looking but pushed her attraction for him to the back of her mind. Emma turned to help Alex bring the boats back to the van but Ben lightly touched her elbow which caused her to stop. She reluctantly turned to face him again.

"So, no chance I might run into you anywhere. I don't want to be a crazed stalker hanging out on this beach all week."

That statement made Emma a little nervous and it showed on her face. She started to back away from him.

"I'm sorry. I was just kidding. I would not do that. I did not mean to make you nervous. I am here by myself so I just thought it would be nice to have someone show me around some more."

Emma relaxed a little. She was suspicious of men these days but she was also raised to be polite. A mental battle was playing out in her mind. Her physical being was attracted to him but her mental being was not interested. He was persistent and she could cut him off now but that would not show good manners. Emma came up with a solution that would benefit both of them. "I did mention that if you order some photos I would hand deliver them to you hotel."

"So, if I was staying at the Blue Dolphin what time do you think you would be there?"

"Since that is towards the end of the strip I think I may be there around seven."

He flashed another one of his killer grins. "Thanks, I really enjoyed myself today."

Emma watched him go wondering what she had gotten herself into.

When they arrived back at the house Emma left Alex to the task of putting the trailer with the boats back in the garage. She went inside and saw Allie was talking to the computer. Allie motioned for Emma to join her. When she reached the desk she saw that her mother had chimed in on Skype. Emma sighed as she sat down in front of the screen. It was a mixed blessing that her mother was learning to use the computer. It allowed them to talk more but maybe a little more than Emma could sometimes handle.

"Hi mom," she waved as she passed the screen. She grabbed a dog treat off the counter and tossed it to her dog.

"Hi honey," her mother said back in her usual cheerful self.

"It was nice talking to you, Grace." Allie bid her farewell and moved out of view.

"Emma, are you still paddling boats around?"

"Yes Mom."

"That is no career for a proper woman. Come home and come back to your life. Everyone misses you."

"No, Mom. You are the only one that misses me. No one else cares. We have been over this. I am not going back."

"You are breaking your father's heart."

"I am not listening to this so unless you have some other news to tell me I have more work to do."

"You know I love you."

"I know Mom. Talk to you soon."

Emma closed the session and went about the business of uploading her photos for the day. She studied the black and whites that she had taken of Ben. She did admit that he had quite the body. The varying shades of gray showed off his rippling muscles. From an artist's standpoint Emma thought the photographs were very good but that is where she was going to leave it. She processed the day's orders and laid the new prints out to dry. She took a shower and put on some casual clothes which for her meant jeans, a tee shirt and flip flops. Emma had no intention of dressing up and flirting with Ben. She was going to give him a few ideas on what to do in the area then send him on his way.

Emma saved Ben's hotel for last. She arrived a few minutes after seven. She had gotten to know most of the hotels in the area and she was familiar with this one as well. It was one of the new and nicest hotels along the oceanfront. The lobby was cool, crisp and clean. There were different shades of blues off-set with tones of white and cream that played to the expansive view of the beach beyond the floor to ceiling windows. Emma scanned the sitting area. If Ben was not there she was going to leave the photos with the front desk staff.

After circling the lobby she decided to watch the view for a few more minutes. There was still some light left in the day and the activity on the beach was winding down. Most would be getting ready for dinner at this point but there were always a few that stayed until the last stretch of light faded pulling the water into darkness. She would never tire of watching the waves crash and the birds glide as they gracefully skimmed the water's surface. Mesmerized by the scene a sense of calm settled over her.

Emma's peace was eventually broken by the reflection of Ben in the window. When she saw him approach her stomach started knotting up. She closed her eyes for a moment trying to calm herself. There was really no reason she should be nervous. She focused on the business at hand which was the photographs. She handled much more difficult business meetings in the past so this one should be easy. She would show him the photos, say good night then be on her way.

Ben was watching Emma from a distance. He could tell that she did not come dressed to impress him. He did not mind. He thought she looked quite fine in her skinny jeans and body hugging tight tee shirt. He was used to woman overtly flirting with him and he admitted he was a big flirt himself. He had learned to tone it down with his last relationship but he still ended up hurt and betrayed. Ben was trying to be more particular with his choices and a part of him was still hopeful the right woman was out there for him. He was not sure if it would be Emma and he could not quite figure out what his attraction to her was but he surely wanted to find out.

Not wanting to get caught watching her, Ben finally decided to approach. He turned on his charm hoping to get to know her a little better or at least get her to agree to another meeting. She sensed him coming and when she turned to him he did a quick reassessment of the situation. She seemed a touch nervous, not wanting to make eye contact. The last thing he wanted to do was scare her away or make her uncomfortable.

"Hi Emma." He smiled at her but kept some space between them. He watched her take a quick deep breath and noticed an instant change in her demeanor.

When Emma took that quick deep breath she kept reminding herself to just think business meeting. She could handle this; she could ignore his good looks and charm. She took a step towards him and held out her hand. "Good evening Ben."

Ben hesitated for a moment slightly bewildered with her sudden change in attitude. He definitely would be watching her closely gauging her interest in him which at the moment seemed to be none. He was still hoping to change that. He shook her hand noting that her skin was warm and silky smooth despite the fact that she paddled a kayak for a living.

"I appreciate your order Ben, shall we have a seat and take a look?"

"Sure." He had to make a quick decision on the type of seating. Should he pick a couch for them to share or go with individual club chairs? The chairs were spaced too far apart for his liking. Instead he found a small table with two chairs set in a small alcove. Ben led Emma over that way and pulled out the chair for her.

Emma sat down and decided to get right down to business. She was not interested in casual conversation. She pulled out the photos he ordered. There were five in all, one of him and four nature shots. She spread them out on the table for him to inspect.

He looked at each one. "You have a good eye. Were all of these taken today?"

"Yes, I try to make it so they are true to each trip. It makes the memories more authentic."

Emma was glad he liked the photos but her nerves stirred up again. She was not sure how he would feel about the next set she was about to show him.

"I have another set of photos for you. I took these of you but I did not post them on my website." Instead of spreading them out on the table she just handed him the envelope. Ben took it from her having no idea what to expect. Her business cool was fading. He looked at her for a moment longer but Emma looked away. He pulled the photos out of the envelope. He had no idea how to react when he saw a series of black and whites of himself. He wondered if this was still all business. He was encouraged that she did see something in him to make a study out of him. Ben noticed she was fidgeting waiting for him to comment.

He picked up one photo pretending to study it with a critical eye. Then he smiled and said, "yeah, I look good."

Emma could not tell if he was joking or if it was part of an over-inflated ego. If the second was true, she surely did not want to encourage it. "I thought, I mean," Emma stammered. She had to get it back together. "It was purely done as an artistic study of motion. Since they are of you, you have a right to the photos. I may want to use them in the future though but I need your permission. If you don't mind can you sign this release?" Emma pulled a document and pen out of her bag and slid them across the table.

Ben was a having trouble following the odd twists and turns of this meeting. He was willing to go about business for a few more minutes but then he was going to shift the conversation. "I have no problem with you using these. What do you think you would do with them?" He signed the release and slid it back to her.

"Basically I am trying to build my overall portfolio but I could see them used in advertising or for portrait work. In any case, I just want to keep my options open."

Ben was glad that was out of the way. "Do you want to join me at the bar for a drink?"

"No thanks, I am good." Emma did not want to put herself in a position where she would lose control of her emotions.

"Well, would you like a drink? I can order something and bring it over here?"

"No, really, I am fine." She watched him sit back crossing his arms over his chest. Emma could not tell if he was irritated with her for turning him down. She could not help if the timing was wrong for her. She felt a little bad. He kept watching her, probably trying to figure her out. She felt a part of her brain wavering. Emma needed to finish her business there and get out.

She pulled out a few brochures from her bag. "I don't know what you like but there are lots of great things to do here. There's the aquarium, some different museums, a zoo, amusement park, dolphin tours, jet skis."

"What do you recommend? I was hoping to get a local's opinion."

"Honestly I am not really a local; I have only been living here since January. I have not been to any of those places."

"Would you like to? Maybe we can do something together?"

"Unlike you, I am not on vacation and I need to work."

"You don't have any tours scheduled on Tuesday or Wednesday."

She could not argue that, at least not without lying and she was not going to do that. He was just so persistent and she was not sure how she was going to dodge this. Maybe she should not. She was wavering again. "Those are my weekend days and I usually work on my photography and my website. I also have the usual housework, shopping and laundry."

"I get your point but how about food? Everyone needs to eat."

Damn, he was not going to give up. Well if he was offering a free meal then why not? It would be better than having him show up at the kayak launch.

"Fine, you can take me out to lunch tomorrow. Be ready to go at 2 o'clock." Emma watched a smile creep across his face. It was a little too smug for her liking. She was still uneasy with the way he looked at her all the time. On the other hand it also made her feel good even if she had no idea why he was interested. In any case she had no problem with a free lunch. Emma got up from the table with him following her towards the door.

"Thanks again for delivering the photos in person."

"No problem," she responded back in a business mode. "Oh, by the way, you should wear long pants and shoes tomorrow if you have them."

Ben looked at her curiously but decided not to question her which may lead her to back out. "Sure, will jeans and sneakers work?"

"Yes, see you tomorrow." She turned and walked back to her van. As Emma was heading out she saw Allie coming in getting ready for her night shift.

Allie headed over towards Emma, "hey roomie, dropping off pictures?"

Emma nodded without making eye contact. She was so bad at hiding stuff.

Allie looked at her, "anything else you want to tell me?" She was getting a little concerned for her friend.

Emma gazed at the sky before she answered, "a guy on my tour this morning really wants to see me again."

Allie was relieved, "so are you going to see him?"

"I agreed to lunch tomorrow."

"Good." But Allie could sense a hesitation. "Don't be so surprised a guy is interested in you. You are smart and beautiful and you need to realize that about yourself."

"I know, I just don't know if I'm ready yet."

"Sometimes you don't get to pick the time or the place. Just don't let the opportunity pass. In any case, it's just lunch."

"You are right. Have a good night." The friends hugged and went their separate ways.

Chapter 3

Ben spent the next morning, first in the gym then, lounging by the pool while catching up on emails and finalizing some details of various work projects. The sun felt good on his bare shoulders. It made him miss home. He felt that New York was just a layover in his life journey. He was not sure where his next stop would be though. He wondered where Emma was from and if this was meant to be her new permanent home. Ben knew nothing about her except that she was tough on the outside but he could sense a vulnerability about her. He hoped to bring her true personality out. He saw glimpses of her passionate and fun side during their kayak trip. She seemed so nervous around him. Ben was not quite sure how to deal with that but he was glad she finally agreed to go out with him.

After showering he put on jeans and a fitted tee shirt. He did have sneakers for running on the beach. Even though it was hot he would have preferred to wear shorts but he trusted Emma's request. He ran a comb through his hair, grabbed his wallet and room key and headed to the lobby just a few minutes before two.

Since Emma seemed adamant that he be on time, Ben decided he would wait outside for her. He did know that she drove a van to haul the kayaks but had no idea if she would arrive in a different vehicle. He leaned against the building watching as some families arrived in minivans packed full of toys and pillows. Others were packing up their cars heading home after a long weekend. Some couples looked as if they were just waking up after a long night of partying. Ben remembered those days well but he was trying to live a different life these days.

A rumbling noise caught his attention. A black and hot pink Harley Davidson motorcycle came ambling up the driveway. There was obviously a female driver. She was alone with no other bikers following behind. He watched out of curiosity as the biker pulled up towards the front doors. He kept one eye on the mystery woman on the bike while the other watched for Emma. The bike stopped and the woman turned to face him. She took off her helmet and when he saw her honey blond hair fall to her shoulders he took in a sharp breath. Her skin tight jeans and black boots gave him an instant rush of heat coursing through his body. This was a complete surprise; a good one he thought but also wondered how many more he would be in store for.

Emma had bought the bike partly out of practicality as it saved her gas money. She really bought it out of rebellion; it was one of her first purchases she made when she arrived at the beach. Her whole family hated when she got her license and now she was free to ride. She loved how the warm summer air rushed past her body. Mostly she loved her sense of freedom and peace when she just went wandering the back roads by herself. It was a deliberate decision to show up with the bike. Either Ben would hate the idea and she could be rid of him or he would be totally turned on by it. She had not truly thought about how she would feel if he was turned on. It did not change her plan either way. She was going to be aloof, have her meal and drop him back off.

She took her helmet off and shook out her hair. She smiled inwardly at the look of shock on his face when he realized who she was. But then he looked at her from toe to head and she realized he had a decided look of hunger for her. She turned away and took a deep breath. She pulled her spare helmet off the back seat and stepped off the bike.

"Do you ride?" She asked a still dazed Ben.

"Um, no," he managed to stammer out.

She gave a cool glare, "not that I would let you drive it anyway. Hope you don't mind being the passenger," she added as she handed the helmet over to him. But before she let go of it she said, "unless you don't feel comfortable."

43

Ben held her gaze. Her cool stare meant that she was trying to scare him off. Well that was not going to happen. He tugged on the helmet freeing it from her grip. "No problem here."

She raised her eyebrows at him and gave a quick reply, "good."

Emma turned to the bike and hopped on. Ben settled in behind her but he was not sure where to put his hands. Sensing his indecision Emma reached back and grabbed his hands and pulled them around her waist. "You need to hold on."

Definitely no problem with that Ben thought as he wrapped his arms around her keeping a light hold of her hips. He wished they did not have to wear the helmets but he understood the need for safety. He was happy just being this close up against Emma's body. He felt the rumble of the engine as Emma started the bike back up. He tightened his grip on her as they took off out of the parking lot. He was impressed with the ease she had guiding them in and out of traffic. Every time they stopped at a traffic light Ben would either brush a hand over a thigh or give her shoulders a quick rub. He was glad that he actually felt her lean into the pressure of the massage. He expected her to brush his hand away. Either Emma was enjoying his touch or she did not want to let go of the handle bars.

It was a bit more work to keep the bike balanced with Ben on the back. He was a good passenger though, not shifting his weight too much. By the time they made it past the main hotel strip she got used to the added weight and she could fly through traffic with more confidence. Emma had to admit it was comforting having his body wrapped around hers. Ben was like a giant piece of armor protecting her. While she felt he was taking advantage of her inability to let go, Emma did enjoy his little massages when they were stopped.

Emma decided to take Ben to the local's beach where houses lined the beach and bay instead of hotels. She turned down the road that parallels the beach and slowed down. The houses ranged from old ranch style nestled in protective dunes to massive multi level mansions. While a few people lived there year round, most of the homes were rented out during the summer on a weekly basis. The atmosphere there was more relaxed and casual than it was by the hotels.

Her destination was a small restaurant at the end of the road. She may not have done many of the things on the list she gave Ben last night but she had actually eaten there and the food was good. She pulled in the parking lot and let Ben get off the bike first. Emma locked the helmets onto the bike and led Ben inside.

The restaurant was small and casual. There were dark woods with surfboards and old time beach pictures lining the walls. Most of the lunch time crowd had already cleared out so they did not have to wait for a table. When they were seated Emma picked up the menu even though she knew what she wanted. She pretended to study it just so she would not have to look at Ben. She still had no idea what to do about him and she did want to give off any conflicting vibes.

After they placed their orders Emma kept her hands on the table while looking around pretending to study the old pictures. When Ben leaned forward sliding his hands towards hers she pulled back setting her hands on her lap instead. He also sat back in his chair but she could tell he kept his eyes on hers. Emma glanced at him quickly as she took a sip of her soda. Ben was still watching her. She had no control over that but she could control what she said to him, if anything at all. She was content to sit in complete silence. She had no intention of starting a conversation. She could already feel the start of an unwanted physical attraction. She did not want to learn anymore about him which would cause her to like him on a more intimate level. Emma gave Ben an icy glare and looked away crossing her arms.

Ben chuckled softly to himself when she turned away. He caught the icy glare but he knew she was starting to melt ever so slightly. She was trying hard to resist him but Ben could tell he was starting to win Emma over. While he generally did not mind silence he decided to try to get a conversation started.

"So where are you from?"

Emma thought for a moment. She could either make up some story, although her reason for moving was almost talk show worthy, or she could give out just enough information to keep him happy. She decided to go with the latter. "New Hampshire."

"What brought you to Virginia?"

"I needed a change of scenery," she stated matter of fact.

"Do you like it here?"

"So far."

"Do you have family here?"

"No."

Emma obviously was not giving out details Ben thought to himself. He decided to change tactics and see if she would ask about him. "I am not from New York. I mean I live there now but I am not from there."

"No kidding." But she said it in a 'that's obvious' manner. When he gave her a quizzical look she added, "The accent is not right."

"What, I could have grown up in Brooklyn," he said in his not so great New York tough guy accent.

Ben caught an almost grin from Emma. Not a full laugh at his attempt to humor her but it was something although she did not ask where he was from. "I lived in San Diego most of my life."

Emma nodded back but did not ask for an explanation. "I took a job transfer." Again, no response. "I'm an architect." She just continued to nod at him but he was not going to give up. "Do you ski?"

Why did he assume that she knew how to ski just because she was from New Hampshire? That fact that she did was beside the point. "Yes, do you surf?" she asked with an edge of sarcasm.

Victory! He got her to ask a question. He smiled at her, "yes as a matter of fact I do."

Emma was glad that at that moment the food came. Her hamburger was cooked to her liking. She took big bites of it not worrying about the barbecue sauce dripping from her lips. She was enjoying her burger and she had no qualms about it. Ben was eating hot wings and licking the sauce off his fingers.

He was actually glad she had no problem making a mess and he was glad she was not shy about eating in general. It also meant that he could eat his wings, not in a total slobbish manner, but he could get away with not using a fork and knife. The sauce was exceptional so Ben could not help licking his fingers as well.

They finished their meal, and since Emma was not interested in dessert, he paid the bill and they headed out the door. They geared back up and settled back on the bike. Ben had the ride home to figure out how to get Emma to stick around a little longer. As she took them out of the parking lot she turned in the opposite direction that they had come from. Maybe he would not have to devise a plan after all.

Emma knew she should just take Ben back to his hotel but it was such a beautiful day. She could use a mental break from work and promoting her business. As long he did not mind the lack of conversation he could tag along some more. Besides, she only told him she would go to lunch with him, she never promised to be good company.

Emma took them up the road to the wildlife refuge. Ben was quick to pull out his wallet and pay the entrance fee when they reached the park ranger booth. She parked in the small lot, locked up their helmets and took out the beach blanket she always carried in her saddle bags. Emma led Ben to a small boardwalk style trail that took them to the dunes and finally up and over the small hills of sand. The beach there was more natural with no lifeguards. There were only a few others set up for the day. There were no screaming kids and she did not have to dodge Frisbees and footballs. While Emma appreciated the tourists and the business they gave her, this was more her style. She could listen to the sound of the crashing waves and the squawking of the birds. There was plenty of space and Emma laid the blanket on the dry sand, keeping a bit of distance from the crashing surf. She pulled off her boots and socks and sat down.

Ben did the same and sat down next to Emma. She watched him as he stretched out digging his toes into the warm sand. She laid back and closed her eyes letting the warm sun melt away her tension. Emma tried to let her mind go blank but she could not stop wondering what part of her brain kept allowing herself to give in to Ben. He was likely going to ask her out again. Why was he bothering when he was only here for a short time? Maybe it was purely out of loneliness but surely there were dozens of single women on the beach that would be willing to keep him company. There was only one other man that ever showed any interest in her but she came here to let the past go.

Emma dug her hand in the sand, picked some up and let it slide through her fingers like an hour glass. Maybe if she stopped wondering why he liked her she could enjoy his company a little more. It was a scary thought for her. She did not trust men right now. If Emma kept careful control of the situation maybe she could in fact enjoy him for a few days. Maybe it would her help her get over her ex-fiancée.

Emma sat up giving her face a break from the direct heat of the sun. For a change, Ben was looking at the ocean instead of her. She sighed thinking Ben was being kind and patient. Most guys would have been bored of her by now. She wondered how you started over in life. She was already doing it by starting her business but what about a personal life. She came here swearing off men but was that really practical?

Emma decided that one gesture, one conversation and one day at a time was what she could handle, nothing more. Since he tolerated her silence for so long she decided to give in a little and talk to him. Emma started pushing sand on his feet with hers covering them up and packing the down the sand. "Do you miss San Diego?"

"Sometimes," he paused, contemplating; "on days like today, at this spot on the beach. The quietness reminds me of surfing early in the morning when there was only a few of us out in the water."

"Not much surfing in New York then?" She shifted her position so she could use her hands to pile the sand higher over his feet.

"There are beaches but they are not so easy to get to without a car."

"When I was a kid," she started as she was now building a wall around the mound of his feet, "we used to go to the beach every summer for a few days at a time. I loved going. It was the only time I felt free to do what I wanted. The rest of the year I was too serious; study hard, join the right club and meet the right people. That is what I heard over and over. At the beach we left that all behind and just had good old fashion fun." She sat back and looked over at Ben. "Do you like New York? Do you think you will stay there?"

Ben was amused watching Emma bury his feet. He was glad she was more relaxed and appreciated that she shared even a small piece of herself with him. He did not think her question went any deeper than a curiosity. He knew she was not thinking in relationship terms but he would move again under the right circumstances.

"I like the city. There is always something to do; some event, festival or parade to check out. However, I don't know if I will stay. I generally think I am open to wherever life might take me. How about you, do you think you will stay here?"

"I don't know either. But I can tell you one thing; you will never catch me in a big city."

If that was a hint Ben got it. He watched her stand up, grab her shoes and decided to tease her a little. "Hey I'm stuck, can you help me up?"

"Poor thing, are your feet trapped?"

"Yes," he said in his saddest face.

Emma grabbed Ben's hand and gave a good yank. As he came up he gazed into her eyes. She felt him coming towards her but she was not ready. Her heart was beating faster and her anxiety building. Emma dropped his hand quickly and in one quick motion she stepped away and reached down to pick up the blanket.

"Hey, I need to stop by my house to see if I have any photos to deliver tonight. Do you mind tagging along?"

"No problem at all." Even though Ben was slightly disappointed he did not get to kiss her he did not take it as a flat out rejection either. Emma opened up to him and was not sending him home just yet. He was happy.

The ride back was just as nice as the ride to the beach. Emma lived a short distance away in a nice suburban neighborhood. She had a cute ranch style house on a tree lined street. After parking the bike in the garage, he followed Emma into the house. It had an open concept with a lot of light but it needed a lot of updating. The carpets were old and worn, the kitchen was all original. Ben was not happy when he noticed another man was living in the house with her. He was also a little taken aback by the large Doberman that was staring him down.

He took a cautious step into the hallway and bent down to let the dog sniff him. Ben figured he could earn extra points by making friends with Emma's four legged protector. He held his hand out for inspection and when he did not pull back a bloody stump Ben started petting her under the chin. He slowly made his way over her neck and shoulder. After a minute she pushed against him giving her approval.

Emma watched in fascination. She had not had her dog very long but she was very loyal and very protective. She also did not like too many men and seemed more wise than most of the human population. The fact that she seemed to like Ben made her feel better. Emma tossed her a treat. "That's Savannah," she said to Ben.

Ben gave Savannah a final stroke down her back and stood back up. When he peeked into the living room he saw a guy that appeared to be a few years younger than him lounging on the couch. In Ben's experience living with someone of the opposite sex was rarely a good idea. It almost always led to a physical relationship. He couldn't stand the thought of Emma with someone else or the possibility that someone might try to make a move on her.

Emma went to the kitchen to drop her keys on the counter. When she turned around to offer Ben a drink she noticed his demeanor had changed. He was standing with his arms crossed shooting daggers at Alex. She was confused but only for a moment. She quickly realized that was a look of possessiveness and jealousy. Her first reaction was to be mad. Ben had no rights to her; there was not even anything going on between them. On the other hand her ex had never shown that kind of reaction when another guy talked to her. Emma had to admit it was kind of nice but she had to diffuse his attitude quickly.

She poured a glass of ice water and brought it over to Ben to help him cool off. "Ben, you remember Alex, my assistant?"

He just nodded in response but he did take the glass forcing his muscles to relax.

"Ben is my roommate's little brother."

He turned to her with eyes still hardened. "You have another roommate?"

"Yes," she said slowly just to torture him. Emma knew where this was going and she thought it was funny. When she saw Ben's jaw clench she decided to ease his mind. "Allie is my roommate; she actually is the assistant manager at your hotel. Alex," she said a little more loudly, "this is Ben. He was on our tour yesterday."

Alex only responded by lifting his arm, "hey man."

Emma sighed, "Alex is enthralled by someone he met on one of our tours. They Skype all the time. Anyway, he goes back to school soon. He's a graduate student."

"Hey Alex, you didn't happen to check to see if any orders need to be printed today did you?"

Alex sat up closing his computer. "Oh, no, I'm sorry."

Emma let out a big sigh. Alex was good for a lot of things but only if you told him what to do. "I'm sorry Ben, I can take you back to your hotel or you can hang out here for a bit while I get this done."

Ben was happy to stay. He relaxed a little when he heard Alex had another female interest. But she was not there. He decided to hang around and dig a little deeper. "No problem. I can wait. So Alex what are you studying?"

"Historical restorations."

Ben was starting to like Alex. "Really? I am an architect."

That got Alex's attention. "Awesome, can you tell me what you are working on?"

Emma watched the two in amazement. One minute Ben looked like he wanted to throw Alex out of the house, the next they were acting like long lost buddies. She let them be and went to her computer.

Emma decided to take Ben back to his hotel in the van. It had been a fairly long day and she was getting tired. They only had to stop at two other hotels before they reached his. He had ordered another photo for himself. Emma wondered if that was his backup plan. Maybe if she did not agree to go to lunch with him he planned on luring her to his hotel every night by buying a new picture. Either way it was a nice gesture.

Emma thanked him and handed him the envelope but she couldn't look directly in his eyes. It was at these times that made her most nervous. She could feel him watching her, feel Ben's desire to lean over and kiss her. Conversation was one thing but a kiss could lead somewhere else she was not willing to go. She kept a tight grip on her steering wheel and stared straight out the windshield.

Ben wished he didn't make her so nervous. He had a nice day and no plans of pushing his luck even further. He did want to see her again. "So what do you have planned for tomorrow?"

She knew this was coming. He was trying to find some other way to see her again. Emma had been trying to decide all day if she was going to include him. "I was going to go out and take more photos of the area."

"Any way I could be of help?"

She hesitated but only briefly. "Sure, why not? Be ready at eight."

He lit up and smiled. He was not even going to try to kiss her, tomorrow was another day. "What should I wear?"

"Shorts, tee shirt."

"Great, see you in the morning," he jumped out of the van and waved.

Emma released her grip on the steering wheel. She wondered when the rational part of her brain was going to overpower this strange physical desire building in her. She hoped real soon.

Chapter 4

Emma was tired when she got up the next morning. Thinking of Ben kept her up for way too long. She was sipping coffee in the kitchen when Allie came through the door. She worked the overnight shifts at the hotel. She was the junior assistant manager so she got stuck with the least desired shifts. Allie and Alex were also new to the area. Allie and Emma lived in the same dorm in college. The timing worked out that Emma was buying the house just as Allie accepted the job offer at the hotel. It was a step up from where she was working before in a small town in Massachusetts. But it was not her final destination; she had even higher aspirations.

"Hey Emma, how was your date yesterday?" They had not seen each other since they passed each other in the hotel parking lot.

"It was nice," but she said in such a way that she hated admitting it.

"That's good, right?"

"Yeah, he's so nice to me so I'm trying hard to be nice back."

"I'm not going to keep lecturing you on that subject."

"I know, I deserve it. Hey, I'm trying. I just don't see where this could go."

"Does it matter right now?"

"I guess not."

"And he's staying at my hotel? What's his name?" Maybe she could give a second opinion or find out more information.

"Ben."

Allie flinched just slightly hoping Emma did not see but she did.

"What was that for?"

"Ben? Tall, nicely built, sandy hair?"

"Yeah," Emma said with caution.

"I met him the night he checked in." Allie was not sure if she should continue. She would not mention how he flirted with her first.

"What are you not telling me?" Emma asked suspiciously.

"Nothing, he seems very nice," but the way Emma was looking at her she did not fully accept that answer. "Look, he's really attractive and I'm sure he's had his share of girlfriends but he likes you and that is all that matters." She let her contemplate that for a moment then asked, "are you going to see him today?"

"Yes, I am taking him kayaking this morning. I decided if he wants to keep hanging out I would make him work for it."

"Good for you, have fun."

Emma pulled in front of the hotel to find Ben waiting for her. She was able to give him a good look as he approached the van. She truly was trying to accept that someone so good looking was interested in her. And she was trying hard not to be so nervous around him. By the end of yesterday she felt more relaxed but she was right back to feeling all jittery especially after Allie's observation of him. She was probably right that he had his share of woman. It would keep her cautious. Despite that there was something else mixed in with the butterflies. It was the start of warmth, a physical desire that Emma had not felt in a long time. Of course that made her nervous too. Emma took a deep breath to calm herself. Enjoy the day and stop questioning she reminded herself.

Emma would have met Ben outside the van except that he was quick to approach. He got in and flashed one of his gorgeous smiles. Her palms were sweating with her grip on the steering wheel and her heart was racing. Luckily her tongue was still working. "Good morning."

"Good morning to you. Did you sleep well?"

Emma replied while she put the van in gear to head out, "I was a little restless."

"I'm sorry. I slept well and the beds here are really comfortable. So where are we going?"

"We are going to stop at the house and pick up the kayaks then head to a creek not too far away."

Ben liked the sound of that. "I thought you did not give private tours," he teased her. But in reality he would hang out with a hundred others if he had to just so he could be with Emma.

"I don't, I'm putting you to work."

"Interesting." Ben was confused though. Was she now just taking advantage of him or did Emma want him to be there with her? Either way it was more time with her.

When they pulled up on her driveway she explained she did not want to wake Alex but she needed help switching out the kayaks. Ben was happy to oblige. He noticed the kayaks they were going to use were considerably nicer than the ones she used on the tour even though those were fairly nice as well.

"These are really nice; they look like they will slice right through the water."

Emma was glad he noticed, "I splurged on these even though they don't get to see the water much. I don't mind that the other ones get banged around a bit but I want to keep these nice."

"Well I feel honored then," Ben said as he slid them on the trailer.

With the boats strapped in place and the trailer hitched to the van, they headed to the kayak launch. It was a short trip which they rode in silence. As they rode through what looked like a typical suburban neighborhood Ben wondered what the waterway was going to be like. They turned off the main road onto a side street that ended in a small parking lot. It was a little more wooded and quiet at the launch. The creek was not more than twenty feet across and surrounded by trees on both sides. They carried the kayaks to the water along with the paddles, vests and coolers. Ben got a little nervous when he saw Emma coming with a pair of machetes. "What are those for?"

Emma tightened her grip on them and pointed them at him. "In case you get out of line," she said in a deep, serious voice.

When he stepped back Emma laughed, "I'm just kidding, but you never know when you might see hairy men playing banjos."

"Um, where are you taking me?" he asked looking around nervously.

"Relax Ben, they are for the snakes."

Now he hoped she was kidding, "seriously?"

"City boy is nervous?"

"No," he answered a little quickly.

"Well just be careful. Sometimes they fall out of the trees." She smiled at him and turned back to grab a few more items from the van.

Ben watched her go. He had no idea what to think and no idea what she intended for him to do. But when she returned he started to understand. Emma was carrying a rope, garbage bag and grabber tool.

"I'm going to tether our boats. You paddle and pick up litter," she handed him the tools to add to his boat, "and I take photographs."

Emma really was putting him to work but he was happy to oblige. It must be hard to paddle and get the perfect photos at the same time. They slid the boats in the water and settled in. Ben noted there were obstacles in both directions but he trusted Emma knew where she was going.

Emma tied her boat to the back of Ben's but left the rope long so she would be able to make adjustments along the way. "You can take us out under the bridge, stay towards the center where the water is low and there are no rocks. I will use my rudder to keep myself centered behind you. Go slow, enjoy the scenery. I will let you know if I want you to stop."

Ben gave her the thumbs up and paddled out to the center of the creek. It was a beautiful day, the sky was a deep blue and there was a slight breeze rustling the trees. The water was smooth as glass perfectly reflecting the scene above. The early morning light was perfect for taking photographs. The heat of the day had yet to take hold which meant the wildlife was still active. The ducks were taking a lazy swim and the turtles soaking in the early rays. Egrets were fishing for breakfast and the elusive great blue herons were flying overhead.

Ben was completely in tune with the surroundings being the perfect guide this time. Since he was ahead of her he would silently point to the local wildlife. At one point he spotted a doe. He held still and quiet nodding in her direction. Emma was able to snap a series of pictures before the doe ran off. Along with all that he did his job in the litter retrieval. Ben picked up tennis balls, water bottles, cigarette packs and whatever else that came along including what Ben thought was a piece of hose. When he went to pick it up he realized it was a snake.

"Oh shit," he screeched as he flung the snake and the grabber into the woods.

Emma broke down in hysterics. Ben, however, did not look amused. Deciding she took enough photos for the day Emma released her boat from Ben's. She paddled alongside him. "Are you okay?" she asked.

"Fine, you weren't kidding about the snakes," he said still a little tense.

"Well at least that one was just a black snake and not poisonous."

He slowly turned his head to her, "there are poisonous snakes in here? You did not tell me that."

"Ben, relax, it is pretty rare for a snake to bite around here."

"I just don't like snakes." He looked off into the woods where he threw the snake. "I will buy you a new grabber; I'm not going into the woods to get it."

"That would be littering."

"I'm fine with it, it's not in the water." He turned around and started heading back in the direction they came.

"Ben, wait up," she called after him. When Emma came along side him she grabbed a hold of his paddle so he would stop. "Ben, is there something wrong?"

He put his paddle down not wanting to get into a tug of war with her. He was not really mad about the snake situation, she did warn him after all. Still there was something he needed to know. While he was happy to be there if it helped her out, he really wanted to know if that is all he was there for. "Emma, is this only reason I am here? Not that I mind helping you out, I was just wondering if you might have any other interest in me?"

Emma sighed as she fiddled with her paddle. Her chest was tightening and the nerves were coming back. "No Ben," she said forcing herself to look at him. She saw the disappointment on his face. She realized she answered his second question. "I mean I do see you as more. It's just that I still feel nervous around you."

Ben was relieved but he was not sure how to make her feel better. "I don't want you to be nervous around me. I like you Emma and I don't know what will happen from one day to the next, I just want to enjoy your company."

Emma felt better knowing there would be no pressure. She leaned over and traced her fingers down his arm and picked up his hand. She loved his hands, they were big and strong. They were protective hands. She intertwined her fingers with his. Her butterflies were once again being replaced by warmth and desire.

Ben was basking in her warmth. He understood that she was giving him a sweet and tender moment. He stayed motionless and silent as the boats slowly drifted with the current. Emma brought his hand to her face. She rested her cheek in his hand and closed her eyes. He sensed there was something more going on but Ben did not want to break the tranquility of the moment. Unfortunately his body was not responding the same way as his brain. The smoothness of her skin was sending electric pulses up his arm and down his body. Touching her face made him want to taste her sweet lips. But as he started to lean over to kiss her, Emma sensed his movement and pulled back.

Emma felt safe with Ben but when she saw him moving closer to her it was an automatic reaction to jump away. She was also not yet sure if she wanted him to kiss her. Her body said yes but her brain shouted not yet. She took Ben's hand in both of hers and looked back at him. "If," she paused, "if something were to happen between us, it would have to go slow. I mean really slow." She squeezed his hand, let go and waited for his response.

Ben was far from disappointed even though his attempt at a kiss was rejected for a second time. This time she at least gave him the thought of possibility. He leaned slightly towards her without crowding her. "Slow works for me." He was glad to see the last of the tension leave her. "By the way I really do hate snakes."

Emma smiled back at him feeling a bit of relief. They paddled back to the launch at a crisp pace without any further interference from snakes.

Back at the house, Ben and Emma loaded the kayaks back in the garage. The temperature was rising to a hot and heavy simmer. The heat was slowing Emma down. She thought of all the things she should be working on. There was bookkeeping, checking reservations, working on her portfolio. Even though she did not book tours seven days a week, she still worked every day. She was torn, she had to stay on top of things to keep her business moving forward but what could a few more hours hurt?

"Hey Ben, did you bring your surfboard?" It was one of the few things Emma had not yet tried and she thought he could give her a lesson.

"No I don't have it. I actually left them in San Diego."

"Oh well, how about some boogie boarding? I have a couple boards floating around in here."

"I am not sure I can balance on something so small," Ben commented with a grin, "but for you, I am willing to give it a try."

Emma found the boards and tossed them to Ben to put in the van. "You can come in. I am going to change and make us some lunch."

Emma went inside and started making sandwiches. Savannah was sitting at her feet waiting for a nibble to fall on the floor. She tossed a piece of bread her way thinking she had no idea what Ben liked. But then if he did not like what she made then he could buy something. She was not going to worry about it too much. As Emma was packing the cooler, her computer chimed in. She sighed, it was her mother on Skype again.

She accepted the call but when she saw her mother she wished she had ignored it. Her mother had an unusual amount of make up on. Emma sighed again and she just looked at the screen with her eyebrows raised.

"Hi honey," her mother said in a cheerful voice.

"What was it this time?" Emma asked her mother.

"Oh, the makeup, the funniest thing happened. I was baking cookies for the church and I dropped the egg on the floor, which of course I slipped on, then hit my head on the cabinet door, which of course was open since that is where the garbage is. You know the one under the sink?"

"Sure mom, whatever you say."

"It's true this time."

Emma just stared at her not knowing what to believe. Not that it mattered anyway. "Nothing else hurt?"

"Nope," she stepped back to show her all of her limbs were in good working order.

"Well, I am getting ready to go to the beach. Anything you need to tell me?"

"Oh. I just wanted to mention that I saw Justin at church the other day. He really misses you."

Emma tensed up at the sound of that name.

"I miss you too, Justin and I both want you to come home and your father too."

Ben came in through the garage door just at that moment. Emma was tired of hearing the same crap over and over and she did not want Ben to hear. She decided to cut the conversation short. "I told you mother, I am not coming home. And I told you never to mention that name again. Good bye mother." She flipped the computer closed without waiting for a reply.

Ben did hear just enough of the conversation and he was worried about Emma's sudden change in demeanor. "Everything okay?" he asked her as reached down to give Savannah some ear rubs.

"Fine, my mother misses me. That is all. Here take that," Emma handed him the cooler. "I will be right out."

Ben did as he was told but he knew she was covering up something. He decided he would wait outside. She did not indicate for him to come back in anyway. She must be changing. He wondered if Emma would come out in a two piece bikini. He wondered how he would be able to control himself if she did. He was getting heated imagining her in all different types of swimwear and outfits. When she did come out a few minutes later he was relieved and only slightly disappointed. Emma was wearing a royal blue racer back one piece with hot pink board shorts. Of course she still looked hot in it and Ben's body reacted accordingly. Still he wished she would show off a sexy, flirty side. Although if she did then twice as many guys would be looking at her and he did not want to deal with that either.

When they got to the beach Emma set up at the chairs and umbrella that were reserved for the week for Ben while he ran up to his room to change. Emma could already feel the sweat trickling down her back so she picked up her boogie board and headed down to the water. Ben came up right behind her and they splashed into the water together.

The ocean was warm but refreshing and the tide was starting to come in which meant there would be plenty of waves to catch. There were also jet skis and boats out in the water that would also make waves.

"Hey Ben, remember, you don't stand up on these. Stay lying down." She jumped up on her board to demonstrate. She looked back at him with a big grin.

"Very cute, I think I can manage your little Atlantic Ocean waves." And just as he said that a wave broke right on him sending him tumbling to the ocean floor which then sent Emma into hysterics.

"Good job surfer boy," she yelled out to him as he came up. She caught the next wave and rode it all the way to dry sand. When she went back out she had an idea. "I bet I can ride the waves further in then you can."

Ben looked at her for a moment pretending to contemplate. He was always ready for a little competition. Maybe he could make this work in his favor. "I will take you up on that bet."

Emma thought he was a little too confident and she was ready to show him up. He may be the better surfer but she was sure she could beat him at this. "Great, what shall we play for?"

Ben had a wicked grin on his face. He was thinking about what he would like to see her in. "If I win, and I will win," he emphasized will, "you have to dress up. In a dress, hair done, makeup, shoes and have dinner at a nice restaurant with me."

Emma gave him a slightly hurt look. "You don't like how I dress?"

Ben bored into her eyes and said in a sultry voice, "I like you no matter what you are wearing."

Emma held his gaze but only for a moment. The comment sent a tingling through her whole body. She ducked under an oncoming wave to cool herself off. She took a deep breath and focused on the game again. "Fine, but you won't win." Emma knew how to dress up but she had not been interested in impressing anyone since she moved to the area. "And when I," she emphasized I, "win, you will have to mow my lawn and pull my weeds."

"You're on."

"We have to ride the same wave for it to count."

Ben nodded in agreement. When the next decent size wave came they both started swimming ahead of it. Emma managed to keep just in front of it which gave her a slight advantage over Ben. She surged forward but then something grabbed her leg. She saw Ben fly in front of her and she knew it was him. When he stopped just in front of her on the sand she kicked water at him, "you cheated."

Ben laughed, "we only agreed to ride the same wave." Ben stood up and raced back into the water.

Emma grumbled, well if he wanted to play dirty then she would too. The little competition turned into a game of bumping and shoving and grabbing. But it was all in good fun as they laughed every time they came up from being tossed into the water.

After a fast round of five consecutive waves, Emma decided to take a breather. She dove under a big wave and when she came up she laid back on her board letting it carry her over the swell of the waves. She closed her eyes letting the heat of the sun warm her face. She had not felt this relaxed in a long time. She admitted she was having a good time with Ben. She was even allowing herself to give in slightly to the physical desire that was stirring inside of her.

Emma was letting her mind go blank when she felt a ripple of the water near her. She opened her eyes to find a hand coming towards her face. She reacted immediately to the unwanted intrusion. She grabbed the arm at the wrist and shoved it real hard away from her head. She sat up and she realized it was Ben's hand. She let go real fast and jumped off her board. She felt really bad; it was just a natural reaction for her. She looked at Ben and saw a wild look of confusion on his face. "I'm sorry. I was dreaming," which was sort of true, "I did not realize it was you."

"I did not mean to startle you. There was seaweed on your face, I was just going to get it off," then hopefully taste those sweet and salty lips he added to himself. She looked so peaceful lying there. They were having a lot of fun. This was the person he knew Emma could be. She had such strange moments of fear and anxiety then moments of pure fun and relaxation. He was pretty sure it was not all related to him. Not with that reaction. That was full on protective mode. There was something going on that she was holding back but he decided to let if go for the moment. It was also another near kiss. Oh well, he was pretty sure there would be more opportunities.

Emma was still a little rattled but she kept her external calm. She needed a break. She started swimming in dragging her board behind her. "I'm hungry, are you coming?"

Ben jumped on his board just in time to catch a wave. When Emma came splashing up next to him he declared, "I win."

"You're still cheating," she said kicking some water at him.

Back at the chairs Emma gave Ben a sandwich and a drink. She was still feeling good about the day. She happily realized that she was not feeling any nervousness even though she did try to pummel him in the water. She was glad that he seemed to have taken it in stride. But he won't want to hear that he lost the bet. "So Ben, I'm pretty sure I won." She flipped her legs over the side of the lounge chair to face him.

Ben tossed his sandwich wrapper into the cooler and returned the gesture so their knees were touching. "I don't think so. I won fair and square." He put a lock on her eyes.

She glared back at him. "More liked crooked." He inched a little closer causing a new surge of heat to race up her legs.

"So how do we decide? Shall we have a tie breaker?" He leaned in towards her lowering his eyes to her lips.

Emma was fighting a grand battle. Her brain said to back off but her body held her in place. Before the battle could be decided Ben's lips were brushing hers. It was the softest, sweetest and most gentle kiss anyone ever gave her. Her whole body tingled with desire, a desire for more but she opened her eyes to find that Ben had pulled back. He was studying her, waiting for some sort of reaction. She did not know how to react though so she just sat silently. This to Ben was a giant leap forward. He wanted more, a lot more, but she said slow and he would oblige. He was glad she did not duck out this time. He sat back ready to compromise on their little battle. "If you dress up and have dinner with me I will come do your yard work."

Emma got her breathing under control even though her body was still on fire. It was a good thing they were under the umbrella. She was pretty sure she would have melted if they were under direct sunlight. "Well, I still think you cheated but I suppose that will work. I think for now though I need to be going home."

"I will help you out to the van." Ben was actually glad. He was heated and not from the sun. He needed to get back into the air conditioning and cool his body off.

They packed up, rinsed off the boards and walked around the hotel to the parking lot. After they loaded up Emma jumped in and sat in the driver's seat facing Ben. "I had a lot of fun today which means I have a lot of stuff I have to get done tomorrow."

"I understand," Ben said even if he did not like it. He was the one on vacation after all, not her.

"I was thinking we could do dinner Thursday night. Since I am doing a night tour on Friday I won't have to worry about staying out late."

"What about your lawn?"

"Maybe Friday or Saturday, it's not a big deal really." It was part of Alex's job to upkeep the yard anyway.

There was a brief flash of disappointment on his face but again he let it go. Ben would have liked to see her the next day but he could wait. "Well then, seven, Thursday night, here at the hotel?"

"See you then," she smiled at him as she pulled her legs in and started the van. He closed the door and they went their own way.

Ben entered the lobby letting the cool air drop his body temperature to almost normal. He headed to the elevators when he heard a click clack following him. He turned to find Allie catching up with him.

"Hey Ben, do you have a moment?"

Being the polite person his mother taught him to be he stopped and nodded his head. He hoped he would not have to decline some sort of invitation.

"I want to talk to you about Emma."

He was thrown off guard. He remembered that they were roommates. He crossed his arms. Well if she planned on talking him out of seeing her she would be disappointed.

"Emma is special. She's been hurt in the past and I just wanted to ask you to go easy on her. I mean, if she acts a little weird or defensive at times just let it go."

Ben relaxed a little. "I noticed she could be a little defensive. And I know she's special, she just does not seem know it."

"You are right; she does not know how pretty she is. Emma does not believe she deserves to be treated well."

Ben was starting to tense up balling his hands. "What happened to her?"

Allie lowered her eyes. "That has to come from her and being that she is trying to get over it I would not push her to tell you."

"How I am supposed to help her then?"

"Just be nice to her, be romantic and do things with no expectations."

"I can do that. Thanks Allie. I will take care of her."

"If you win her heart you will be one lucky man."

"I know." They gave each other a slight nod and Ben headed towards the elevator.

"Oh, and Ben," he stopped and turned back, "I'll be watching."

He smiled, gave another nod and headed back to his room.

Chapter 5

The next day Emma went back to her routine of tending to her business. She pulled her best photos and started narrowing down which ones to add to her portfolio. She was also planning to sell her work at some local art and craft shows. Along with that she had to tend to cleaning house and doing laundry. While her roommates were fairly neat Emma felt the house was ultimately hers and her responsibility. She liked for it to be kept neat and clean which meant most of the chores fell on her.

Concentrating on her chores was the actual chore. Ben's intense eyes and soft lips kept creeping into her mind. It also did not help that he was still ordering photos from her and the photos of him kept popping up on her screen.

When she got just enough work done to satisfy her she went to the kitchen to contemplate dinner. She was the only one that cooked in this house. She did not mind most of the time since she generally liked to cook. Her mother taught her early on and she also liked to experiment with new recipes. The alternative, if left to Allie and Alex, would be takeout every night and they would all be overweight. Tonight was one of those nights that take-out would be a good possibility. Emma opened the refrigerator anyway to see what her options were. They were running low on food so she would have to scrape something together.

She was still staring when she heard Savannah starting to whine. She looked over to find her at the door circling as if waiting to greet someone. Emma was curious since her dog generally warned people away. The doorbell rang before she got there and Savannah let out a little yip.

Ben was standing at the door with two paper grocery bags in hand. She opened the door before her dog broke though the glass. "Hi Ben, I thought we were doing dinner tomorrow."

"We are." He walked past her into the kitchen. He took a big rawhide bone out of the bag and gave it to Savannah. She responded by wagging her stub of a tail and rubbing on his leg. Ben put his bags down and gave Savannah extra attention by getting into a mini tug of war with her. Ben let her win and then she settled down at his feet to start chewing on her prize.

Emma still could not get over how much her dog loved him and she still wondered why he was in her kitchen. "So what's up Ben?"

"I", he started pulling groceries out of the bag, "am cooking for you tonight."

"Why?" Emma asked with her usual suspicion.

Ben stopped for a moment. He remembered what Allie had told him. "No reason, do I have to have a reason?"

Emma looked at the floor feeling conflicted. She was used to cooking and she did not often let people in her kitchen but he was trying to be nice, "no, I guess not."

"Good, now go away, I will take care of everything."

"But what if you can't find something." Cooking was one thing but letting him rummage through her kitchen was another.

"I am sure I can manage."

"But . . ."

"Go," he shooed her away. "I will let you know when it is ready."

"Alex and Allie are here too. I need to make them something to eat."

"I got them covered. Go away," he said with a cheerful smile and wave of the hand.

"Fine." She was out of excuses. "Come on Savannah," but her dog just looked from Ben to her whining. Emma stalked off, even her dog was no longer loyal.

Emma heard him opening cabinets and drawers and then the banging of the pots and pans started. She had to think of an alternative for dinner. She had no idea if he could cook anything decent or not. Maybe she would call for Chinese takeout if it was really bad. There was no way she would be able to concentrate on work with Ben in her kitchen. She headed to the spare room that Allie used as a den and office. It was her trade off for taking the smaller bedroom. She sat down heavily on the couch sighing.

Allie turned to look at her. "It must suck having a sexy man cooking dinner for you," she commented with a slight edge of sarcasm.

Emma relaxed a little. Her friend was right. Still, how could she trust he would not screw it up? "If it totally sucks we will get takeout after he leaves."

"Why would you assume that?" Allie asked as she was tapping away on her computer.

"I don't know."

"Besides it does not matter if it is good or bad, it's the thought and effort that counts."

"I guess," but Emma wondered what he expected in return. She changed the topic, "so what are you working on?"

"Blue is planning a new hotel in New York City." Blue was the new upscale line of luxury hotels that Allie worked for.

"Do you think you will apply?"

"Probably, but I am sure I will be against a lot of others so my chances will be slim."

"You are great at your job."

"Thanks," she turned to face Emma beaming. "It would be awesome though, don't you think? It's where I really want to be."

"Yeah, it will be great," Emma sighed, "They will love you, hire you and with Alex back at school I will be all by myself."

Allie turned back to the computer. "I am sure Ben will visit."

"Right, he will forget about me as soon he is back in the city with all those beautiful, sophisticated woman."

"Maybe they are not his type. Maybe you are his type."

"Guarded and controlling?"

"No, try fun, hard working and adventurous."

Emma really had no comment for that. She stretched out on the couch and closed her eyes. The rhythmic tapping of Allie's fingers on the keyboard actually relaxed her. She imagined Ben wrapped around her keeping her warm and safe. She dozed off in a blissful sleep.

Emma had no idea how much time passed when she was awakened by a bell. Or at least she thought it was the ringing of a bell. She could just as easily been dreaming it. In any case, Ben announced that dinner was ready.

Emma did a full body stretch before getting up. She took a deep breath taking in the aroma from the kitchen. It was definitely some kind of seafood but she was not sure what else. She strolled over to the kitchen to find Ben putting the finishing touches on the plates. It was nice to see the old table covered in a new tablecloth. The silverware was laid with care in its proper place. There was also a vase with pink roses. She did notice that there were only three place settings. He did say that he had Allie and Alex covered. She wondered who he would possibly invite to eat with them.

"Just three settings?" asked Emma.

"Oh, I'm not staying," Ben replied as he opened a bottle of wine and placed it on the table.

Emma was not sure if she should be disappointed, she was still mostly confused by the whole situation.

Her confusion must have been obvious. "This is just for you, Allie and Alex. We will have our dinner together tomorrow."

Allie and Alex came in the kitchen with big grins on their faces. The trio took their places at the table. Ben commenced serving them salad followed by the main course. Normally he would have spaced out the two but he did not want to hover. The main course consisted of grilled salmon, rice pilaf and roasted vegetables. He finished by filling the glasses with wine. "There is cheesecake in the fridge for dessert. Enjoy," he gave a slight bow and left them alone.

Emma watched him leave still bewildered. Ben did not even press her for a kiss. When she turned back her roommates were looking at her with big grins. "What?"

Alex was digging into his food. It was a simple meal but perfectly prepared. The salmon was tender and juicy, the rice steaming and vegetables just lightly seasoned. In between bites he said, "You should definitely keep him around."

"What, you don't like my cooking?" Emma snipped back.

Alex nodded back at her since his mouth was full so Allie jumped in. "Sure we do but don't you like to be waited on every so often?"

Emma shrugged her shoulders as she didn't actually know. She had always taken care of everything which meant things got done to her liking. "Maybe you guys should cook once in a while then."

"You would starve," Alex replied.

Allie gave her brother a little punch on the shoulder. "I could cook but Emma always gets to it first." Allie gave Emma a little wink.

"You burn toast," Alex reminded her.

Emma laughed at the siblings. Even though they bantered back and forth they watched out for each other. Emma wished she could say that for her own brother. At least she had Allie and Alex here now. They continued eating and enjoying each other's company.

After dinner and dessert the two ladies settled back in the living room while Alex did the dishes. That was the other advantage to cooking Emma reminded herself, someone else usual did the cleanup work. They poured another glass of wine and talked about their day and the people they met.

When they ran out of conversation Allie looked at Emma, "what do you plan on wearing tomorrow?"

Emma sighed, she was still undecided. "I am not sure if I should go summer dress sweet or short and sexy. I don't think he will care either way." Emma remembered his comment. "Although he did tell me to dress up."

"What do you want to wear, what would make you feel good?"

Emma fidgeted for a minute contemplating. "I really want to do the sexy thing."

"So what is the problem?"

"I'm afraid of where it might lead." Emma bit her lip and looked away.

"Emma, look at me. Has he done anything that you have not wanted him to do?"

"No, he said he would go slowly."

"He's a good man, you have nothing to worry about."

"I am not sure I can pull it off."

"Of course you can." Allie got up but turned back to Emma. "Wait there."

Emma did as she was told. She was warming up to the idea of getting dressed up. In her old life she wore skirts and heels all the time but it was all business. She was starting to plan how she could put her hair up and paint her nails. When Allie came back into the room her eyes lit up. Allie was holding a short, shimmering dress. It was covered in silver fringe that shimmered under the lights. She also had a pair of silver strap heels that would lace partly up her calves.

Emma got up, hand over her mouth. "Where did you get that dress?"

Allie smiled at her, "I might have gone shopping earlier today. Consider it a returned favor for letting us live here, cooking for us and cleaning up after us."

"Allie, it's beautiful. And these shoes are perfect."

"Ben is going to love it."

Yes he will, Emma thought and she was actually looking forward to seeing his reaction.

Back at the hotel Ben was sitting on the couch in his suite flipping channels. He was greatly satisfied with the events of the evening. It had been a risk just showing up at the house with no warning. Of course the fact that the dog liked him played very well in his favor. He always had dogs growing up but they were never pure breeds. His mother would take in any scruffy mutt that needed a home. Eventually he would get a dog of his own. Living alone in the city he did not feel he would provide a dog with enough attention.

Thinking of his mother made Ben miss her more. She heavily protested when he left their hometown but ultimately understood his decision. They were still close and talked frequently. As if she sensed him mentally, Ben's phone rang and it was his mother.

"Hi mom," he said.

"Hi Ben, how is your trip going?"

Ben smiled, "its going well mom. Thanks for talking me into going."

"I knew it."

"Knew what mom?"

"Love is in the air, my love chimes were blowing in the wind today. I thought I would check to see if it was you. So who is she?" She inquired without checking to see if she was right.

Ben laughed to no one in particular. His mother was into a variety of spiritual things but mostly she burned incense and hung spirit chimes. She was also a hopeless romantic. His parents had a great relationship. While his father did not believe in most of his wife's readings he was more than willing to humor her about it. Ben's thoughts were generally in line with his father's but he too played along. "I went on a kayak tour and she was the guide."

"What else?"

"Not much else mom," he did not want to get her hopes up. She hated when he was younger, never keeping a girlfriend for long. And the one he did keep she never liked.

"We have spent some time together and we are going out to dinner tomorrow."

"Oh Ben, I just knew there was a reason you were meant to go on this trip."

"Well, I don't know what is going to happen but thanks mom."

"I have a good feeling about this Ben. Good night."

"Good night mom." Ben hung up hoping his mother was right.

Chapter 6

Allie and Alex decided to forgo the bar scene the next night and went to the movies instead. Emma was left alone to shower and get ready. She preferred it that way. She did not want to be fussed over. After she showered and painted her nails she sat on her bed looking at two dresses. One was the short flirty dress Allie bought her, the other was a long flowing summer dress. The first one said I am ready to pursue you, the second one said I am still not ready. But was this really just about Ben or about life in general? Was she ready for Ben or any relationship? Was she ready to believe she was worthy of this dress? She also remembered what Allie told her, that it was more about what she wanted.

An hour later Emma was stepping out of a cab in front Ben's hotel. She opted not to drive as her nervous butterflies were coming back in full force. She really wanted to have a drink. She paid the fare and went inside.

By the time she got half-way across the lobby she was starting to feel self conscious. There were too many people looking at her. She started to think she had made the wrong choice. By the time she reached the host podium for the restaurant she was debating on turning back.

"Can I help you ma'am?" the host asked Emma pulling her out of her thoughts.

"Oh, I, um, am meeting someone here."

"Name?" he asked with a slight edge of impatience.

"My name is Emma."

"Ah yes, Ben is waiting for you, follow me please."

Emma walked around the podium then grabbed the host on the elbow. "Do I have something on me? On my face or something?"

"I don't see anything." He turned and kept going.

Emma caught back up. "Are you sure, I feel like everyone is staring at me."

The host stopped and turned to face Emma. He looked at her from head to toe. "Honey, if you did not want to be looked at you should not have worn that dress." He turned and kept going.

Emma was not sure if he meant that in a good way or bad but before she could ask they were at Ben's table. And before she knew what was happening Ben had his lips on hers. She stiffened in shock but when he pulled her closer she melted into his body.

When Ben felt her relax he pressed even harder against her. The swell of her breasts sent a rush of heat right down to his core. He wished he could skip dinner and whisk her away but he did not want to overstep his boundaries so he took one last taste of her sweet lips and let her go. He stepped back to take a closer look at Emma. He had caught glimpses of her as she followed the host to his table. He had no idea what to expect and he pictured her in many different outfits but this one topped everything. He took in her lean, long legs, narrow but curved hips and breasts that perfectly complimented her athletic body. As he looked into her blue eyes he could not imagine how she did not realize how beautiful she was. He noticed that she looked slightly uncomfortable as they took their seats. "You look amazing."

Emma felt Ben's gaze on her. It was like two little lasers sending a burning path from her toes to her head. It also woke the jittery butterflies in her stomach. She took a deep breath to quiet them down. She really wanted to enjoy her evening with Ben. It was a nice compliment and one she did not hear very often. "Thanks Ben, I have to admit though, I feel a little self conscious. I kept checking to see if I had toilet paper stuck to my shoe." She chuckled which actually helped put the rest of the butterflies to rest.

Ben leaned forward and said in low sultry voice, "well, I certainly wanted to make sure everyone knew that you are spoken for."

Emma held his gaze back. "Is that right?" She did not recall agreeing to any sort of relationship but she was not mad. Actually it made her feel good that he was showing a little jealous side.

"Yes that is right. Do you have a problem with that?" he countered back.

Emma sat back picking up her menu. "No."

"Good." Ben sat back smiling at her. "How do you not know how beautiful you are?" Ben genuinely wanted to know.

Nervous butterflies were waking up again, "when you are told all of your life that you are plain Jane you start to believe it."

Ben was surprised, "who told you that?"

"Mostly my dad. Then when I started working out in college my mom chastised me. I looked too tough, no man wanted a girl stronger than he was and when I did find someone that liked me I was supposed to feel lucky no matter what he was like."

"Maybe your dad was just trying to keep you from dating," Ben said half joking. But Emma was not laughing. "I'm sorry, that was pretty shitty. Every girl is supposed to be a beautiful princess to their dad."

"I need a drink," Emma said to no one in particular while she studied the menu. That was as much as she wanted to divulge about her past right now.

Ben could tell he made Emma uncomfortable and remembering what Allie told him he decided to change the topic. "Do you want an appetizer?"

"No, I would rather save room for dessert."

Ben smiled, "I like the sound of that."

Emma shot him a little dagger. "I don't mean you, I had something better in mind," she teased him

"What could possibly be better than me?"

"One word: chocolate!"

Ben contemplated for a moment but then he realized he could not argue the point, maybe a little later on he could but for now, "I concede. Of course if you combine me and chocolate..," he gave her a wicked grin.

Luckily the waitress came before Emma had time to get too embarrassed over that one.

Emma ordered a filet mignon with a Blue Hawaiian. Ben ordered shrimp scampi with a Sam Adams. Emma had no plans of sitting in silence that evening. She wanted to keep Ben talking. But she wanted to hear about him. Eventually she would have to tell him more about herself but for now she wanted to know more about Ben. "So what did you do today?"

"I worked out, did some laps in the pool. I checked my email, talked to my mom, showered. How about you?"

"Pretty much the same, did my tour this morning, checked email, showered. Luckily my mom did not bug me today." She quickly turned the conversation back to him so he would not ask about her mom. "Tell me about your parents."

"My parents are the happiest, in love couple I know. My mom is a hopeless romantic and she is into all things spiritual. As a matter of fact she called to tell me her love chimes were blowing."

"Love chimes?"

"She has a series of wind chimes and each one stands for something different and yesterday it was the love chimes."

"So she assumed it was related to you? Or maybe it was how much Savannah likes you."

Ben laughed and said, "You know moms, always wanting us to settle down."

"Have you had many girlfriends?" She was pretty sure she knew the answer but somehow it seemed important to hear what he had to say.

That was a tough one for Ben to answer. He thought about he wanted to say. He wanted to be honest with Emma but she might not like what he had to say. "Not a lot of girlfriends, a lot of dates but not too many serious."

Emma just nodded in response knowing he might say something like that. It was part of her reason for not understanding why he was so interested in her. But she had to stop questioning. The real question was, would she be able to hold on to him knowing there were always women ready and willing to be with him. Despite her concerns she wanted to keep the conversation light. "So I bet your mother was not too pleased with that."

Ben laughed, "No, she is always getting on me to settle down."

"I know not now, but did you eventually?"

Their drinks came and they both took a good long drink. "I did, but obviously it did not work out."

"Is that part of the reason why you left?"

Ben picked up his beer bottle, looked out in the distance and took a swig and nodded his head.

"Can I ask what happened?" Emma asked softly grabbing his hand.

"Carla and I worked together. Office romances were discouraged but we dated anyway. I really thought she was going to be the one and I contemplated buying her a ring. One day she was up for a promotion. It was really difficult not to recommend her but the other person was the better choice. She went insane, she started accusing me of sexual harassment."

"That really sucks. That must have been hard to deal with."

"Unfortunately my old dating habits came back to haunt me. Because our relationship was not completely out in the open it was hard to fight it. Then it just got hard to go to work every day. I was told I could go quietly or transfer. So I left."

"Do you think the accusations would have followed you if you stayed in San Diego?"

"I guess I did not wait around long enough to find out."

"How long have you been in New York?"

"About a year."

Emma was sympathetic but she was also curious about the past year. "Any girlfriends since then?"

"Nothing long term. I have been trying to build my career back up."

Emma was partly glad to hear that. She was glad that he was focused on his career. However, he did not say he did not date at all. She picked up Bens hand. She held the backside and pulled it to her cheek. She closed her eyes taking in its warmth. She kissed his palm then let to go. "Do you have any siblings?"

Ben shook his head no.

"I see why your mother was upset that you left."

All during the conversation Ben had been keeping a watch on Emma's reaction. He had not been sure what to expect. He knew she had some confidence issues but she seemed to be getting better. She held his gaze taking in his words. It was not a superficial gaze he often received from women. She was paying attention to him beyond what he looked like. While he could not totally tell what she was thinking Emma did not seem to be judgmental and even sensed sympathy. That was something he had not experienced in a very long time. Feeling the soft skin of her cheek sent a sense of peace over him. He wondered also what it meant that she kept doing that. He was not going to ask though, he just savored the tender moment.

Their meals came and they both ordered a second set of drinks. They savored their dinner in silence while picking off each other's plates. Emma's steak was tender and juicy without being over cooked and Ben's pasta had just enough sauce to not be overwhelming.

As they were nearing the end of the meal Ben started the conversation back up. He wiped the sauce from his mouth, "so I noticed your house could use a few upgrades."

Emma laughed at that, "what, you don't like the way it is?"

"Sure, if you like seventies style."

"Well mister design guy, what would you recommended?"

"The structure appears to be good so it's all cosmetic. It's whatever style you like."

"I had not given it much thought and I have been fairly busy. Maybe after the summer season is over I can think about it. I do know the carpets will have to go first. But I don't know. I can swing all the supplies, it's just getting the work done that is the problem."

Ben looked at her with a slightly sinister grin. "It just so happens that I know how to install flooring and countertops and paint walls and cabinets." He had been wondering how to approach the subject of coming back to visit without scaring her off and this would be the perfect excuse.

Emma had a feeling where this was going but she was not ready to decide on the course of this . . . this what? It was not a relationship, not really a fling. She did like Ben but had no idea how to handle a long distance relationship. She sighed and remembered what she told herself, one day at a time. She focused back on Ben who was still grinning at her with his eyes. "Is that right? I thought you just drew the pictures," she teased him.

"I built things before I drew them. I still have a few tools lying around."

"Well I will have to keep that in mind," she said with no intention of making any commitment.

The waitress came by to take their dessert orders. Ben declined and after Emma ordered a slice of chocolate cake she requested hers to go.

Ben was a little disappointed, he did not want the dinner to end. He decided he would pay the bill and offer to go for a walk on the beach. He figured that was a nice romantic ending to dinner that most women liked. "Do you want to take a walk along the water? I can put your cake up in the room real quick?"

"Actually, I have never seen the view from high up. I would love to see it from your balcony." Emma knew he would take her up, but she did not want to give him the wrong impression. She still intended to take a cab home. Or maybe she would stay. She was enjoying Ben's company and the alcohol was giving her a warm buzz. So that is why she would have to leave, before she did anything she regretted.

Ben led Emma out of the restaurant with his hand on the small of her back as if to stake his claim. At first Emma was inclined to push his hand away not liking the possessiveness it insinuated. She was also fighting a feeling of being controlled. She was already breathing a little harder when Ben moved his hand to her shoulder. She casually ducked to the side just out of his reach. She pretended something caught her eye over at the bar and what she did find was a group of college boys eyeing her from the top down. She immediately felt bad for making assumptions about Ben. She realized he was not trying to control or even possess her but was protecting her. Since she clearly was with Ben she thought the blatant staring to be rude. She quickly edged back to him and took his hand and smiled a thanks.

Ben wanted to slap every one of those boys as he passed by. A glance is one thing but he knew those looks of animal desire very well. He used to be one of those guys and now that he was on the receiving end he had to make a big effort to keep walking. He had been so focused on the boys that he barely noticed Emma moving away from him. When she grabbed his hand and smiled at him his anger quickly dissipated. He melted at her smile in the shimmering dress. He felt like a little puppy dog following his owner around.

They rode the elevator hand in hand but also in a comfortable silence. Ben led Emma down the hall to his suite. Emma went inside first and quickly headed to the balcony doors. As much as she wanted to inspect the decor and amenities she did not want to linger and give Ben any romantic ideas. Of course going up to his room in the first place probably was sending him the wrong signals. She would take a brief look outside, take in the view of her new found home and then call a cab.

After a minute of investigation Emma managed to unlock the balcony door and stepped outside. She took a deep breath inhaling the salt air. There was a breeze coming in that gave the air a slight chill. Emma rubbed her arms out of habit but she was not really cold, not after living her life in the north. She looked up and down the lighted boardwalk. There was still plenty of activity. Families pedaled surrey bikes, couples walked hand in hand and others wobbled their way on roller blades.

The beach had alternating stripes of light and darkness depending on which hotels had rooftop spotlights. The light of the moon created a sparkle on the tips of the waves just before crashing on the shore. Emma was mesmerized by the thundering rumble that even the smallest waves made. She stood at the railing letting the power of the waves free her mind.

Ben watched Emma from inside the room. He wanted to give her a few minutes alone. He was not exactly sure of her intention for the evening. She genuinely seemed interested in the night scene but was that all? Of course he wanted her to stay the night but that was purely selfish. He only had a few more days and he wanted to spend as much of it with Emma as he could. When he saw her run her hands up her arms he had a plan.

Emma was not sure how much time had passed when she felt the warmth of Ben's arm on her shoulder. She smiled and realized that she did in fact feel a little cold. She wanted to fully lean into him but was afraid of losing control of her feelings. "I could listen to the sound of the waves all night. Do you ever leave the door open at night?"

"That would let out all the air conditioning," Ben softly replied while rubbing the chill off her arms.

Emma turned and smiled, "I have had enough of the cold. And I need to call a cab." She managed to maneuver out of Ben's arms but before she could pull out her phone Ben pulled her back slightly.

"Follow me, I want to show you something." Ben took Emma's hand and led her to the bathroom.

Emma was confused but she would indulge Ben for another minute. She was even more confused when she ended up in the bathroom. Ben turned her to face the tub. She stared at the inches of soothing bubbles sitting on top of steaming water. There was a hint of lavender in the air that was sending out calming vibes.

Ben pushed Emma's hair to the side, "stay a while, take a long, hot bath and relax. You deserve it. I will also bring your cake in here for you."

Emma smiled, she could not remember the last time she took a bath, probably not since she was a kid. And Ben did another nice thing for her. "Chocolate and a bath, how can I resist?" She turned and gave Ben a soft kiss on the lips, "thank you."

"You are welcome, take as long as you want." Ben brought in the cake and a bottle of water and then left her alone.

Emma undressed and slid into the warm bubbles. She sunk down low letting the white foam form a beard under her chin. She played with it making shapes then blew them across the tub. She felt good being silly again even if was just for a few minutes.

After finishing off the decadent, chocolate cake she sat back and closed her eyes. Her skin started to tingle as the bubbles slowly popped from the heat of the water. It reminded her of the way Ben made her feel every time he touched her. She imagined what it be like to have his hands running up her legs and over her breasts. She ached to have his lips on hers again. She was already hot from the water but her thoughts were causing her blood to almost boil over. She sat up and ran a small stream of cool water and splashed it over her face.

Feeling better she sat back but her thoughts were still on the man waiting for her. She knew that he would eventually ask to see her again after he left but she had not thought yet how she would respond. Besides, her not feeling ready for a relationship she was also not sure about the long distance aspect. And to add to it, she knew his history of dating. She would have to learn how to trust him, she would have to learn how to trust herself and believe that she was worthy of him. He had been nothing but kind and patient and she was enjoying the attention. She would wait on deciding the future but she did have to decide on the rest of the evening.

Ben had changed into his pajama pants and a tee shirt after Emma closed the bathroom door. He stacked up the pillows on the bed so he was in a more upright position and flipped on the television. He was absentmindedly scrolling though the channels when his phone beeped. It was a text from a woman he had taken out once. Or was it a few times? He could not remember. It seemed that she was looking for someone to hang out with. He wondered if he was her first choice. Probably not at this late hour. There was a time he would have dropped what he was doing, happy to entertain one of the ladies. But now he had no interest. He started scrolling through his list of contacts and realized he had no interest in any of them. Emma was the only person he wanted to keep on his list. He started scrolling through and deleted anyone he could not quite remember or did not want to see. He almost stopped for a minute feeling like he was deleting memories from his life. He had settled down once but the relationship ended badly. He pictured his ex girlfriend then Emma. He imagined her smooth and silky skin. He wondered which parts were peeking out from under the sea of bubbles. He was getting hard thinking of the red tips of her nipples and her pink scrumptious lips. He wanted to bury his face in the bubbles seeking her out, tasting every part of her. His phone beeped again interrupting his fantasy, it was the same woman. He sent a brief out of town message and shut the phone off. He was considering the possibility that Emma could cause him to try a long term relationship again, certainly his body thought so. He got up to get a drink of water to cool himself off. He was not sure how long Emma would be in the tub and he did not want her to see him in his heated state.

When he sat back down the bathroom door opened a crack. Emma popped her head out, "hey Ben, do you have a spare shirt I can wear?"

He grinned at that. He was tempted to say no, that she would have to be naked the rest of the night but that would more likely cause her to call a cab and go home. He grabbed one of his old favorite San Diego shirts thinking she would look cute in it.

Emma held her hand out through the cracked open door and grabbed the shirt. It was old and gray and very soft. She held it up to her face and took a deep breath. The shirt smelled like Ben. It was slightly musty mixed with the scent of cool breeze. She felt like a giddy school girl who would forget to give the shirt back, hide it in her dresser and never wash it.

She laughed at herself and put the shirt on. She was glad it was long enough to cover her bottom as she obviously could not ask for shorts to wear as well. She looked at herself in the mirror and instead of seeing a giddily school girl she saw a woman with a body that any man should appreciate. It was the first time she looked at herself in that way. Emma was beginning to realize she could attract men and that she did not have to settle. She thought about Ben and how he was always telling her how beautiful she was. She was starting to believe him and it made her feel good. But was he the one for her, knowing that there were others out there that would likely take an interest in her if she tried? Ben sure has tried out a lot of women, maybe she should do the same. Ultimately though she did not think she was capable of that. Going back to being single seemed easier, but lonely as well. She had to stop trying to decide her future.

She stepped out of the bathroom and quickly made her way over to the bed before she gave Ben too much of a show. She slid under the covers, pulled them up to her chin and pretended to be interested in what was on the television.

Ben smiled as Emma jumped into bed. He did manage to catch just enough of a glimpse of her to keep his brain occupied. What mattered more though was the fact that she seemed to want to stay the night. He rolled over on his side to face her. He pushed the hair off her face, "how was your bath?"

"It was relaxing, thank you. Between the bath and the drinks I am so relaxed I did not think I could make it two steps out the door. And being that this is a hotel and all I figured I would just sleep here, if that is okay with you?"

Ben leaned in close, "you are not going anywhere." He caressed her cheeks with his thumb and closed the final half inch by taking a taste of her lips that he had been dreaming of. He started slow but then demanded more by pulling her whole body closer to him.

Emma tensed slightly at first but quickly relaxed enjoying the weight of his body on hers. She held his head rubbing her hands through his hair. Her breathing deepened causing her breasts to push against his chest which in turn made him press harder on her lips, sweeping his tongue across hers. The electricity was racing through her and she felt herself losing control of her rational self. Emma stiffened slightly and pulled back to catch her breath.

Ben took the hint. Before he pulled back he showered her with mini kisses across her lips and eyelids. He felt bad that she tensed up and told her to roll over. "Trust me," he said when she glared at him. After a brief second she gave in and shifted the pillows so she could lie on her stomach. Ben sat up and moved to the end of the bed. He picked up Emma's foot and started his intended full body massage. He started with each toe slowly moving his way to the ball of her foot then her heel.

Emma sighed and closed her eyes letting every last bit of tension flow out of her body. She let her mind go blank so she could just enjoy the feel of Ben's strong hands rubbing away her physical and mental aches. Every time he moved to another part of her she wished he would go back yet silently begged him to stay in the new area. As he moved across her body Emma was fighting to maintain focus. No one had ever given her a massage and she wanted to enjoy every second of it but her mind was slipping into a peace she could not ever remember experiencing.

Ben could feel Emma relax and he was glad that she let herself go. Of course he was enjoying exploring both her athletic and feminine aspects of her body. He knew when she drifted off to sleep but finished the massage anyway knowing that it would still do her body good. When he was done he turned her on her side and curled his body around hers and drifted off to sleep.

Chapter 7

Emma stretched as her brain struggled to focus. She generally woke up at the same time every day so she knew the time but something was not quite right. As her eyes opened and the fog cleared she remembered she was still at the hotel with Ben lying next to her. She turned over and watched his broad chest rising and falling for a few minutes before quietly slipping out of bed. She headed to the bathroom first then made her way to the balcony. Since she was up she decided to watch the sun rise. She pulled a chair up to the railing and took in the morning view. The sky was slowly releasing its grip on the darkness as the edge of the sun began to exert its power on the horizon. There were a few clouds streaking across the sky and as the sun rose higher the clouds exploded in brilliant pinks and oranges. The ocean was also coming alive with an array of blues. The waves were more demanding; rumbling at a faster pace on the shoreline. As the new light was bringing life to the new day, the early risers were also starting their day. The waves brought the surfers and the cooler air the morning joggers, while the chairs and umbrellas were being readied for the day's beach goers. As more people came out Emma decided she needed to head back inside to relax a little longer.

Emma did not want to disturb Ben by climbing back in bed. She was also too awake to try to go back to sleep. She quietly closed the sliding door to the balcony and closed the door to the bedroom as far as it would go without clicking it. She stretched out on the couch and turned the television on. She aimlessly changed the channel looking for something that was not news. She settled on a movie she had seen multiple times since it would not require her to concentrate on the story line. Her mind was more on Ben. He had been so nice and patient. Everything about the previous night had been perfect. The dinner, bath and massage were all amazing but she could not imagine how long it would last. Considering his history with women she was not sure how long his patience would last. Especially when he went back home and was surrounded by more beautiful women again.

She was half tempted to quietly get up and leave but there was something else that was keeping her. It was a little pull on her heart strings that kept her glued to the couch. It was the sense of comfort, peace and security she had with Ben. She thought she had that with Justin. Of course looking back Emma could see how slowly his control took over her life. She was not sure she trusted not only Ben, but herself. While she was not nearly as nervous around him she was still learning how to respond to his generosity. She felt like she was always in jeopardy of doing or saying the wrong thing and, as much as she did not want to hurt Ben, she was scared that it was inevitable.

As she was laying on the couch trying to decide what to do about the situation Ben appeared in the doorway. He was looking a little scruffy as he rubbed his hands through his hair. Despite his needing a shower and shave he still looked sexy. When Emma's eyes travelled down his midsection she noted the hint of desire for her. She closed her eyes and took a deep breath. She wondered if this was his normal for any woman or was it really for her. She hoped the latter and it sent a tingling through her own nerves. She was still struggling with her body saying yes please and her brain saying no way.

She opened her eyes when she heard Ben ask her, "do you want to come back to bed? You can watch the movie in there."

"No. I am fine here," she replied thinking the bed was not a safe place for her right now. The hotel room, as a whole, was probably not safe but at least he could take a little more of a hint if she stayed put. When he disappeared back in the bedroom she thought he was going to go back to sleep but instead he came out with a couple of pillows. He tossed them on the couch and squeezed his body behind Emma's. He wrapped his whole body around hers, throwing his leg over hers and wrapping his arm around her chest holding on tight to make sure she did not leave. Emma stretched out grabbing his arm. She basked in his warmth. That is what she liked the most, feeling his body around hers forming a protective bubble. Melting into his body, Emma drifted back into a peaceful sleep.

Ben was very content as well. Emma asked nothing from him and there was no pressure. He did wish she would ask for more, more of anything would be fine. He would keep doing nice things for her without asking for anything in return. But when he thought about it he was already getting a lot in return. He got to be with a beautiful, intelligent and determined woman. She had no expectations and did not judge him. The question now was to figure out how to hold on to her. He also had to figure out how to keep his strong physical desire for her in check. He did feel that she wanted him also, there was a definite spark passing between them but she had much better control than he did. Right now he would settle for holding on to her, keeping her warm and keeping her safe from her demons.

His dreams were a different story though. There was no control; it was only what his body wanted. And what his body wanted was to be one with Emma. His body was so heated when he woke up, and it was not from laying next to her. She had moved to the other end of the couch and was sitting with his legs over her lap. When he opened his eyes, Emma was looking at him but she was not quite as relaxed as she had been. He truly hoped he had not tried to make any funny moves on her while he was sleeping. He sat up and brushed his hand across Emma's cheek, this time without her swiping it away. He brushed his lips across hers. He looked into her eyes and saw them soften ever slightly. That made him feel better. He smiled at her. "Good morning," he told her as he got up and went to the bathroom so he could tame his desire for her.

Emma watched him walk away wishing she had the guts to hang on to him and ask for more. She had moved from him when she felt his desire for her pushing against her thighs. It scared and thrilled her all at the same time. She never felt such a strong pull for someone and wondered why she never felt that way about Justin. Sex with Justin had been frequent but that was it. This surge of emotions, desire and heat she kept feeling with Ben was new and she was not sure how to control it or if she even wanted to learn. Either way, he would be back in New York in a few days and she would have more space and time to figure it out. For now, she had the excuse of needing to go home and tend to her business.

Ben returned after freshening up and cooling down. Emma was still a little flush and she could not look at him. She gripped her hands together to try to distract herself. When he sat down next to her she instinctively shimmied away. She was hoping that he did not notice but she knew he did and she felt bad. She felt Ben's hand pry her hands apart. After a split second she let go but she kept her eyes closed. She did relax a little when she felt his hand come up her arm and across her neck giving her a small massage.

"Did you sleep well?" he asked her quietly.

Emma's head was lowered in response to the neck rub but she did manage to nod a yes.

"Everything all right this morning? You seem a little tense."

Emma bit her lip but gave him another nod yes, but it was not very convincing even to Ben.

"You know you can talk to me about anything," he told her as he pulled her hair away from her face. He saw the conflict on her face. He kept softly rubbing her head hoping she would take it as an invite to open up to him.

Half of her wanted to run but Emma was still so drawn to his touch. Maybe she should talk to him, she really did not have anyone else. Her mother and brother were no help and Allie was understanding but felt she should be over Justin by now and she did not feel as comfortable talking to Alex. Emma took a deep breath to gather her nerves but kept her eyes lowered. "How long will you wait for me Ben?"

"I told you, as long as you need," he said softly wanting to reassure her.

Emma finally looked up at him. She was far from reassured though and it showed on her face with her eyes slightly squinted and eyebrows pressed together. "Really? Because Ben you have needs and I am not sure if or when I will be ready to deal with that." She felt

Ben pull away from her but she went on. "It's obvious you want me and, well, I am glad you are attracted to me but I am not ready to deal with it." She waited nervously for his response. She glanced at his face, he looked almost shocked.

"What do you mean, deal with my needs?"

Emma wished he had understood her, maybe he did but obviously she needed to clarify. "Sex, Ben. Men need sex and its part of my job to keep you satisfied." Keep you from straying she added silently to herself.

Ben was in shock. He could not believe he was hearing this. He was not mad, well maybe he was at the person who made her believe that. He was also sad for her, he wondered if anyone had made love to her. He understood a little more why she was nervous and shy around him, but a part of him was having trouble believing that was how she really felt. He pushed her hair back one more time as he gently turned her head to face his. "Is that what you think? You feel like you have an obligation to have sex with me?"

Emma knew Ben had not intended it but she sort of felt ashamed and now confused. "I don't know," said really quietly. "I mean, that's kind of what my mother told me when I moved in with Justin." In her mother's voice she repeated what she was told, "if you want to your man to stick around, keep him satisfied. Even if you are not in the mood, just let him do his thing and he will not wander."

Now Ben was angry but he could not let it show. He did not want to judge her mother but he could not believe she would say something like that. "Emma, I would never, ever do that to you. I want to make love to you, not just have sex with you. I want to make every inch of your body tingle, I want to light a fire in your soul, I want our hearts to beat together as one. I want both of us to feel like there is no one else in the universe."

She heard the words, she liked the words. But was he sincere? "Is that how it is with every woman you are with?"

That stung Ben a little but she was right and she had a right to know. "No."

"So sometimes it is about sex and satisfying a need."

Ben flinched, she was hitting a sore spot with him and this was not where he intended this conversation to go. "It was not always about me you know, women have needs too."

"And you were happy to help out," she stated matter of fact. "Are you telling me all this so I can be another notch on your bedpost?"

"No, that is not what I want."

"What do you want from me then? You come down here, sweet talk me into hanging out with you and soon you are going to leave. Then what?"

"Well, I want to see you again. It's not a far drive and in between we can talk, text, Skype. I want us to be a part of each other's lives." He moved back closer to her and took her hands back in his.

"I don't know if I can give you what you want." She started to get up but he held onto her hands and pulled her close to him

He pulled her so their faces were only a few inches apart. He looked through her eyes and into her soul so she would feel his words. "You are what I want. No one else, only you." He paused before adding, "and I will wait."

"How can you know that already?"

"Because I can think of nothing else when I am with you and when I am not with you I think of no one else. Because of you I deleted every female contact in my phone and left only yours." He closed in on the last inches separating their lips. He ever so softly put his lips on hers. He was seeking a response that would tell him if he could continue. She parted her lips and he pressed harder. Ben pulled her body tight against his as his lips pressed harder. His tongue sought out hers and he took in her sweet taste and scent. As much as he wanted more he remembered patience and pulled back.

Emma gasped when he pulled back. Her lips were swollen from the heat and electricity flowing through them. And it was not just her lips; her whole body was tingling right down to her toes. She did not know what to do now or how to respond. She jumped when she heard the phone ring next to her. She breathed a sigh of relief, glad for the distraction. Before Ben could stop her she reached over and picked up the receiver not caring who might be on the other end. "Hello?" she said as she watched Ben sit back rubbing his hands through his hair in mild frustration.

"Hello, may I speak to Ben please?"

Just as Emma was about to hand the receiver over, she suddenly realized who it was. "Allie, is that you?"

"Emma?"

"Why are you calling Ben? Aren't you at home?"

"No, I got called into work. Haven't you been watching the weather?"

"Um, no, I have been a little preoccupied." Normally she kept up on it so she could make adjustments to her schedule but she really had only paid attention on a day to day basis this week.

"Well yes, apparently you have been busy."

Emma could tell she was grinning ear to ear but she was going to ignore that for now. "So what is going on?"

"It looks like a hurricane is heading this way. Right now it is forecast to hit south of here, move over the area and then swing up the coast then back out to sea."

"I thought it was not supposed to come this way." Emma recalled something about a storm out in the ocean.

"Well it turned so now it looks as if we are in its path."

Emma groaned in response while she felt around for the remote to turn on the weather channel.

"Listen Emma, Alex is going home to help mom and I am stuck here which means you will be by yourself."

Emma did not like the sound of that. "Can't I stay here?"

"No, as a matter of fact we are trying to get as many guests as we can to check out. Emma, ask Ben to stay with you."

Emma contemplated for a moment twirling the phone cord around her finger. She finally found the weather channel and watched as the storm swirled slowly in the Atlantic. "I don't know, I am sure I can manage but I will let him know about checking out."

"Please think about it Emma, I would feel better if someone stayed with you."

"All right," she responded without committing either way. She hung up the phone and focused back on the weather forecast. It appeared that it would still be clear for the next thirty six hours which was good for her tours.

Emma's thoughts were interrupted when she saw Ben emerge from the bathroom. She had not noticed that he had left.

"Who was on the phone?" he mumbled as he was brushing his teeth.

"You need to check out early."

"What? Why?" he asked from inside the bathroom.

Emma pointed at the TV, "there's a hurricane heading this way. The hotel is asking everyone to check out early."

"What about you, you are not going to stay are you?"

"Where would I go? Besides I still have a business to run. I have tours scheduled that I have to deal with."

Emma got up realizing there would be a lot of details she had to sort out and needed to think about getting home.

Ben jumped up as well, he was more concerned about Emma than what he needed to do. "Will Alex be there?"

Emma grabbed her dress from the bathroom. She could lie in hopes that Ben would go home but he would likely find out. "He went home to help his mom. She is the caretaker of a house on Martha's Vineyard so he went back to help secure the property."

"I'm staying with you then." He pulled his suitcase out of the closet to start packing.

Emma was getting a little irritated. Who did he think he was? He was not going to invite himself over without at least asking. "That's not necessary, I will be fine."

Ben stopped for a moment to face Emma. "There's a lot to deal with, not just your tours but stocking up on food and securing your yard."

"I don't need your help," she said with an edge to her raised voice. And she did not need anyone taking control of her life.

"I want to help you." Ben growled back at her. He started tossing more clothes into his bag.

Emma slipped her dress back on but she felt overdressed so she put Ben's shirt over it and tied the bottom into a knot. She did not want to argue, she just wanted to get home and figure out what she needed to do. "You can take me home," she said a little more softly as she grabbed her shoes and headed to the door.

Ben drove her home as requested. Neither one spoke, both afraid of saying the wrong thing. Ben wanted to give her some time to cool off. He was sure she would calm down. He was not sure if she would come around and let him stay but he had another day to work on that. When he pulled into her driveway he did tell her that he would be back in a little while to check in with her.

Not that she had any choice she grumbled to herself. Ben would come back no matter what she said so she did not try to argue. She just nodded and headed inside. Savannah greeted her enthusiastically, tail nub wagging as only it could. She kneeled down giving her a great big hug. Savannah obliged her by putting her head on Emma's shoulder. Dogs were so much easier Emma thought. They only asked for food and a pat on the head and they were happy. Relationships were too much work. She never knew if Ben wanted something in return or if she was acting properly. She sighed, she should stop worrying. Ben never had a problem with anything she said or did. Enough of that for now, she headed to her computer to start making phone calls.

Two hours later she found out that no one wanted to cancel the evening tour and two people were still up for the next day. She cancelled Sunday and Monday which would leave her Tuesday and Wednesday to regroup as needed. She also checked for any updates on the storm. It was a category two with a lot of heavy rain wrapped around the center. She had lived through many snowstorms but never a hurricane. She finally admitted to herself that it was making her a little nervous and she truly had no place to go and now she had no help with the kayaks. Emma really did not want to ask for Ben's help but she had no choice. Maybe she could get another full body massage out of it. That thought finally made her smile.

When Ben returned two hours later she was feeling better about things. She let him in and he greeted Savannah with a fresh bone which she promptly ran away with. Ben had several bags in his hand and Emma followed him into the kitchen. She watched as he methodically started unloading the packages.

"Flashlights and batteries," he started showing her all the items, "can foods we can heat on the grill, crackers, chips and cookies."

Emma laughed. "Cookies, of course."

'What?"

"Nothing, what are the Ziplocs for?"

"You fill them with water and pack them in your freezer and it will keep the food cold longer."

"Oh, where did you learn that from?"

"I just know things," he replied a little smugly. "Is your grill tank full?"

"I am not sure, it might be half way," Emma replied as she continued to rummage thought the bags. Buried beneath the cans of soup her finger caught on some paper. She pulled out a booklet, Hurricane Preparedness. "You just know things, huh," she tossed it at Ben.

He shrugged, "well I do now."

Emma jumped up on the counter as he put the groceries in the pantry. Her little butterflies were stirring. She needed to ask him now before she lost her nerve. She reached out her hand, "Ben?"

He turned and saw a look of anticipation on her face. He could not help thinking how cute she looked in her nervousness. Ben accepted her invitation and went over and grabbed her outreached hand.

Emma pulled him close, glad that he did not make a fuss, and wrapped her legs around him. She needed to stop being so foolish about him. "I'm sorry about this morning Ben," she started quietly. She worked up the courage to look in his eyes. His beautiful eyes that matched his beautiful grin that made her melt into a puddle of mush. She took a deep breath and continued. "You know this is not easy for me," she paused again, "but I could use your help." She stopped again; her words were not coming out quite right. "I mean, will you help me? I would like you to stay. With Alex gone, I can't believe he just left with no warning, I can handle the kayaks but it would be easier if I had help. I thought everyone would be leaving town but no one cancelled tonight. Which is fine, I still need the money. Even tomorrow I have two that still want to go and looking at the weather it should be fine. It would just be nice to have someone, I mean you there to help me," and just as she was about to take a breath his lips were on her hers. She took him in fully pulling him closer, wrapping her arms around his neck. Her butterflies turned to electric pulses and had she not been sitting on the counter she would have in fact melted into the floor.

Emma was sad and grateful at the same time when Ben pulled back. She smiled at the way his eyes smiled into hers but when she caught the edge of his hand coming at her face she instinctively grabbed at it again. Her eyes flashed emotionless for a split second and she hoped he did not notice. She needed to stop doing that. So as fast as she caught her own actions she brought his hand to her lips and covered it in soft kisses. "So I take that as a yes?" She asked trying to further deflect her slight lapse.

Ben did take notice of her quickly shifting behavior but let it go when her kisses sent waves of warmth through his body. The warmth was much more then lust, it was a deep growing affection for Emma. One he hoped to explore even further over the next few days. Whatever the reason for her change in attitude he was willing to accept it without question. "Whatever you need, I am at your service."

Emma jumped off the counter, "well, wise hurricane preparer, what else do we need to do?"

"Let's see, I will check the tank on the grill, we need to secure or put away everything in the yard. What time do we need to leave tonight boss?"

"We need to be out the door at 6:45."

Chapter 8

Emma led her moonlight tours on a different waterway. It was actually an ocean inlet that got dredged out yearly so the wealthy could take their big boats out to the ocean. The waterway eventually led to a small creek surrounded by marshland. Generally the water was pretty calm but she was worried there would be a stronger current caused by the far away storm. They would not have to venture close to the ocean though. In any case it was more about the full moon rising, the stars and of course the wine. That is why she picked everyone up at the hotels. Everyone could have a few drinks without worrying about getting back and she would not worry about their safety. She also only brought enough alcohol for everyone to have fun but not get out of control. The tour cost quite a bit more but it also filled far in advance and Emma hoped the weather cooperated.

That evening was no exception, there was a slight breeze blowing that would hopefully keep the mosquitoes at bay. There were only a few wispy clouds floating across the dark turquoise sky. The plan was to get everyone settled and comfortable on the water before the moon lit up the night sky.

Ben was doing a great job taking the boats, paddles and vests to the launch. It was a concrete launch used by all types of boats. They would be able to push two people at a time onto the water before joining the group. Tonight's group included a husband and wife, Henry and Alice, visiting their son who was in between military deployments. A second couple, Jake and Erin, having a date night without their young children and the last two were a pair of college graduate students, Ashley and Jill, having a weekend outing before going back to school. Emma would always be the professional but she did not like the girls from the moment they got in the van. They obviously had their eyes on Ben. She did not think he had noticed yet or he was ignoring them but she was definitely going to watch to see how he responded to them.

Emma first went through her basic paddling instructions. "Due to the currents we likely will not go too close to the inlet, we definitely won't go beyond the bridge that leads to the ocean. Once the moon starts rising we will tether together, enjoy our drinks and snacks. There is a cooler in each boat with a small assortment of wine and beer as well as cheese and crackers. Feel free to share and trade. There is also a small flashlight and bug spray. Everything is for you to keep at the end of the night. I will be paddling around taking photos. If anyone runs into any problems just give a shout to either Ben or me." Emma took note of the smile spreading across the girls. Emma hoped they had been half listening to her as they kept their eyes glued to Ben. "Any questions?"

Ashley quickly chimed in, "are there any alligators?" she asked in an innocent sweet girl way.

Emma heard this question a lot and was no longer shocked that people thought they came this far north. She wondered if Ashley was truly curious. She gave her usual answer despite her suspicions, "no alligators or crocodiles here, but there can be snakes although I have not seen any in these waters."

Ashley gave a little shudder, "Ben, you won't let one get in my boat, right?"

Emma silently laughed knowing Ben's fear of snakes.

Ben started handing out the life vests and paddles while he answered, "I would not worry, if you see one just ignore it and it won't bother you." At least he hoped.

"Can you help me adjust my vest?" Jill jumped in taking it from Ben.

Emma watched the scene as the two fought for Ben's attention. He was being a little too flirty with them for her liking. He smiled as he adjusted their straps. He stood behind them with his hand next to theirs on the paddles as he showed them the motion of rowing.

Emma's trance was broken when Alice whispered in her ear, "those are the sharpest jealous daggers I have ever seen."

Emma contemplated that for a moment before turning to the woman. "Well, I don't know if I would call it jealousy being that we are not even dating." Which was true so why was she upset with Ben and where were these feelings even coming from? He was likely just being himself but did she want to get used to that?

"Not dating? Well if I was your age I would be after him," Alice added with a sly smile.

"That's part of the problem; a lot of women want to date him and he's dated a lot of them." She continued to watch as the girls purposely stumbled getting into the kayaks allowing Ben to catch them.

"In my experience guys like Ben eventually settle down. The right woman comes along and steals their hearts forever." She turned and winked at her husband. "And it looks like you have captured his."

"How can you tell?" They only had just met after all.

"While you are glaring at those girls he is sneaking glances back at you." Alice turned back to Emma and in a motherly fashion Emma had never experienced she put her hand over Emma's heart and asked, "So will you listen to what your heart wants?"

Emma was close to tears for the surge of emotions. "What if my heart and my brain can't agree?"

"Always listen to your heart, the brain clips our decisions, over thinking, over rationalizing and before you know it your chance is gone."

Emma watched as Alice turned and kissed her husband before letting Ben help her into her boat. She grabbed her own paddle and vest and climbed in so Ben could push her into the water.

Ben knelt next to her, "everything okay?"

Emma just nodded still undecided over the situation.

"Are you sure?" he asked noticing a slight change in her demeanor.

"Yup," she tried to sound as cheerful as possible, "ready to go."

After Ben caught up, Emma led the group over to the marshy areas. The tide was high enough for them to get fairly close to the shoreline. They watched for osprey and listened as the night creatures started their ritual orchestrations. Ben's admirers continuously giggled as they knocked boats and banged paddles with Ben. Emma happily held the attention of the other two couples as she educated them on the local wildlife. She took advantage of the last bits of sunlight photographing the group as a whole, as couples and individually. And of course the girls wanted pictures with Ben which she obliged.

When Emma spotted the first of the moon rising in the distance she led the group out to the center of the waterway. She had Ben pass a rope through all the boats so they would drift all together. Ben positioned himself with Jill and Ashley on one side and Emma on the other side. That would not have been Emma's choice but she supposed it was the proper thing to do.

The group settled in pulling out their snacks and popping open the wine and beer. Emma had similar coolers for herself and Ben but with water and soda instead of the alcohol. The conversation ceased as the moon rose as an orange glowing ball stealing the glory of the setting sun. The mirror of the water responded to it with a brilliant reflection streaking across its surface. Emma released herself from the group and paddled around taking photos of the lunar show.

As the moon rose it let go of the sun's setting color turning to the silver glow of the night. The sky darkened around it allowing the stars to share in the night stage. Emma pulled her boat back next to Ben's but faced it the opposite way of the group so she could face him. She smiled at him before turning her attention to the stars.

Ben reached over and grabbed Emma's hand. "This is really a great tour you put together."

Emma squeezed his hand, "thanks." She focused back on him, "I really do appreciate your help." With an almost forced smile she added, "even if you are flirting with the clients."

Ben leaned back understanding Emma's slight irritation with him earlier. It was obvious the girls were flirting with him. Of course he was being nice back to them but he did not think it crossed the line into flirting. Ben looked over at Emma, she had a forced look of concentration on her face as she pointed her camera at the moon. A smile slowly crept across his face as he realized that she was jealous. It was not his intention to upset her although Emma was sure cute in her reaction. He leaned over as close as the boats would allow. So the girls would not hear he softly said, "you're jealous."

Emma kept looking at the sky and just shook her head no in response.

Ben reiterated, "You're jealous," he paused then added, "you're cute when you are jealous and you have nothing to worry about. I told you, you are the one I want, no one else. No matter what I say or do around other women you will always be the one I come back to, the one in my thoughts. I know it may not seem like it but I was raised to be a gentleman and I was raised to be loyal." Ben knew they were just words but hopefully his actions would eventually convince her.

Emma shot back, "so does that mean you politely let your dates down?"

Once again Ben knew he deserved that but he was trying and he would show Emma he meant his words. "Well I don't know if I was always polite but I was always honest." Ben thought back to a few of his dates that expected way more than they should have.

Emma silently took in his words knowing in her heart they were true. She remembered Alice's words of advice to not over think things. She smiled at Ben and took another photo of him wanting to capture his sincerity. She did not have a response just yet, so she went back to the star gazing.

After a few minutes multiple hands went up in unison, "shooting star," the group pointed out together.

From the end of the line Henry said, "we should all share a wish or a dream."

Jill responded first, "but then it won't come true."

Erin chimed in on that. "Honey, you don't have to share your inner most wish but sometimes if we say what we want out loud it will give us the courage to go after our dreams." She looked up at the stars for a moment then said her wish. "My wish is kind of simple and Susie homemaker but I would love to be president of the PTA when my kids go to school."

Her husband quickly added, "And I hope to coach my son's baseball team. And I hope to have the wisdom to be a good coach yet separate it from being a good father."

Alice quickly praised them for wanting to be a big part of their children's lives. "I wish for my son to stay safe in the military and always come home from deployment. And I hope to have many more great adventures like this one."

Henry expanded on that, "I hope to have grandkids some day to share our travels with."

Emma was enjoying this. She would have to consider adding this to her other night tours, it was a little like group therapy. She was also pleased at Alice's comment. It was always her goal to give each person the best experience she could. She turned to the girls, "how about you?"

Jill answered first, "ultimately I would love to write and produce a Broadway play."

"That I will star in," Ashley added. Then she looked at Ben with a smile, "what about you?"

Ben had been thinking about how to respond while everyone else took their turn. He knew he wanted

Emma, and he wanted to figure out how to continue their relationship but did not think it was the right time to get so personal. "I would love to buy an old house to renovate for myself, something I can breathe new life into."

The whole group then turned to Emma. She almost did not want to answer claiming that she did not have to as the owner and guide. Then that would not be fair to everyone else. Her life was slowly coming into focus but she was still not truly sure where it would ultimately lead. She did have one thing she could at least dream about though even if was not realistic right now. "I wish I had a house on the water with a small dock so I would not have to take the boats on and off the trailer every day."

Ben listened with great interest. He wanted a house to renovate and she wanted a better location. The gears in his brain started spinning.

After they had dropped the last of the group back at the hotels Ben wanted to know more about Emma's wish.

"I don't know Ben, I don't really see it happening. I do know I have a lot to think about. With Alex leaving soon I'm going need to hire a helper. While it has been a lot of fun it really is a lot of work hauling the kayaks around all the time. When I came here I focused on earning money as quickly as I could. Now I have to think about which direction I want to go. I still want to do the tours but I hope to expand the photography side especially after summer is over. Of course in my ultimate dreamland the house with the pier could even be a bed and breakfast."

"Hold on to that dream Emma because I don't think it is unrealistic especially with your determination."

Emma grabbed Ben's hand, "thanks, for now though, I hope I can stop focusing on one day at a time and maybe move up to one week at a time."

"You will get there, I know you will."

Emma was glad he had confidence in her and with that it gave her a small but needed boost of confidence for herself.

It was only noon the next day when the kayaks were put away. The two men on the tour requested to be back at their hotel a little earlier. It was fine with Emma since the wind was starting to pick up a touch and the first few rain drops were already rolling in. The storm was not due to blow in until the next afternoon but Emma wanted everything secure. Not only did she dread the coming storm but she dreaded the feeling of being trapped. There were a few things she could catch up on but basically she was facing the next 48 hours alone with Ben. Emma knew she should be ecstatic about that. While she was not anxious or nervous it was more of a feeling of obligation to keep him entertained.

While Ben brought in the garbage cans she decided she was not going to worry about it. He made it through their first day together with her barely saying a word to him. She did ask him to stay but he actually offered first so he would have to deal with being bored. He really did not seem the type to sit around and watch TV but neither was she. On the other hand a day of doing nothing might be good.

Emma tossed her purse and cooler in the kitchen when she noticed new text messages. Generally she ignored her phone when she was out on the water and that day was no exception. She did carry it for emergency calls but only if she needed to make a call, not receive one. She shook her head when she realized she had at least ten messages from her brother. It appeared her mother was trying to get in touch with her. They only talked through Skype being her mother did not have a cell phone and was forbidden from making long distance phone calls. Her mother should have known that she was out on the water so she wondered what the urgency was. She went to use the computer in her bedroom to give herself a little privacy.

She knew her mother would be sitting by her computer so she had no problem connecting. "Hey mom, everything okay?" she asked as she went to her closet to change her clothes. There had only been a small water fight this time, mostly between her and Ben so she was just a little too wet for comfort.

"Emma, what are doing there, haven't you been watching the weather," she said in a half frantic voice.

"Yes mother," she yelled back from the closet. She pulled a new shirt on and went to her computer desk. When she looked at her mother her whole body tensed. "Mom, what happened to your eye?" There was a faint purple ring around her left eye, partly hidden by concealer, "that had not been there a few days ago."

"Emma, don't you change the subject on me."

"Well I am not talking until you tell me what happened."

"Oh for goodness sakes Emma, I spilled some water when I was cooking and I slipped and hit my head on the corner of the counter."

"Whatever mom," her mother's face showed no expression and her eyes did not shift with her story. She was either getting really good at lying or developing a medical condition called clumsiness. Emma was pretty sure she was lying and confronting her about it would only cause her to retreat. Emma felt it was better to keep open lines with her mother so she could keep track of what was going on.

"Please tell me you are evacuating."

"No, I'm staying, everything will be fine. Besides I have nowhere to go."

"How can you say that? You need to come home anyway, I have been asking for months. Now is a good time."

"And leave my home, that I own in case you have not forgotten, and my business."

"What if something happens and you can't get out? What will you do then?"

Emma could not help but laugh when she responded. "Well I guess I will just row away on one of my kayaks."

But her mother was not amused. "What about your roommates, will they be there with you?"

"Well no, but I do have a, um, friend staying with me."

Her mother raised her eyebrows at that, "a friend?"

"Yes." Emma was ready to end the conversation, "listen mom, I have a few more things to do," sort of, "but I promise to check in with you as often as I can."

Not so ironically Ben was also talking to his mother. A mother's concern for her child never ends but Ben's mother had a different outlook on the situation. "It was so strange Ben. The winds just shifted and completely tangled the love, danger, friendship and betrayal chimes all together in one big knot. I have never seen anything like it. The love chimes have been sparkling all week but now I am very concerned for you. I cannot imagine what is going on."

Ben hid his amusement. He loved his mother and always pretended to be interested in his mother's spiritual words of wisdom but he sure would not let them control his life.

"Maybe they don't all pertain to me mom, have you considered that?"

"Yes of course, but they all knotted together. That is what is different this time. It is all about one person."

"Well I would not worry mom, there is a storm coming but we are ready for it." That covered the danger and love chimes, he was not sure about the other two but again, he did not look too deeply into it.

"Ben, this goes way beyond the storm, it is going to take some time to unknot this and I can't do it myself. It's a warning and you need to be cautious."

"Do you think I should abandon this relationship?" Ben almost regretted asking since his mother's answer did not matter. He was not giving up on Emma under any circumstance.

"That is a tough question and one without a correct answer. The chimes are still blowing. I think if she is worth the risk then you need to heed the warning and proceed with caution."

"She's worth it all right. Listen mom, we have a few more things to put away before the next rain comes so I am going to go, I will check in with you."

Emma came into the living room as Ben was finishing his conversation. She flopped down on the couch grabbing one of the pillows to her chest. Savannah had followed her and jumped up on the couch next to her. Emma had no problem letting her dog hang out on the furniture. Savannah had no problem letting Emma use her as a pillow in return for the privilege.

Ben had insisted on sleeping on the couch even though they had shared a bed at the hotel. She did not argue since they had to get up early anyway. Also it was a nice gesture showing that he was giving her the space and time she asked for. She stretched out on the couch throwing her legs over Savannah while also feeling comforted by Ben's lingering scent. Talking to her mother always sucked a little too much energy out of her. Having caught the end of Ben's conversation he wondered if his mother was expressing similar concerns.

"Your mother worried about the storm also?"

"A little," this was not really a lie. Ben did not want to drag Emma into his mother's wind prophecies.

"Yours too?" he asked with his head in the refrigerator. He grabbed two drinks and sat down on the floor in front of the couch. He was not about to challenge Savannah's rightful place next to her owner, at least not yet.

"I don't know if it is the storm so much or just another excuse to get me to go back home."

"She must really miss you."

"I guess, she was really disappointed when I broke off my engagement."

Ben knew he was warned not to ask but he did want to know, "why did you break it off?"

Emma took a deep breath thinking about how to answer. She knew she should give him something. "We started out liking the same things but ultimately our points of view changed and I could not see spending my life with him." While not the whole story it was the truth and Emma was glad when he did not try to dig further.

"Have you been back to visit?"

"No, I need more time." She needed to get the focus off her so she asked him the same question.

"No I have been busy with work." When he said that he realized how lame that sounded, "but I guess that is just an excuse. I have no reason not to."

They both sat in silence for a few minutes contemplating the directions their lives had taken and whether or not they would or could return home. Emma needed to stop thinking about it though. Not only could she not go home she was back to feeling trapped. She threw the pillow at Ben hoping to break his own trance, "I am going to go crazy. Of course there have been days I have stayed at home. I just don't like not having the option and we don't know how long it will last. What are we going to do?" Emma said with a little more force out of frustration.

Ben spun and sat up on his knees leaning in towards Emma. "I can think of a few things we could do." He looked into her eyes not trying to hide his desire for her.

"I bet you do," Emma pushed him back but not before stealing a quick kiss. She smiled back at him to let him know she was comfortable with his teasing, "Seriously Ben, when I was a kid and we were stuck inside because of a blizzard my choices were to read or read. To my parents it was another opportunity for me to study. There were no family games by candlelight or camping in the living room. I was trapped in my bedroom with a flashlight and school books. I hated it."

"Well then I think we need to find something to keep us occupied." Ben got up and started looking around; he walked from room to room with his hand on his chin.

She had no idea what he was doing so she got up and followed him. "What are you doing?"

He stopped and turned to her, "what is the one thing you want to change the most about your house."

Emma was a little taken aback by his question but played along anyway. She looked around as well before answering, "the carpets are nasty. I want to be able walk around barefoot. I am thinking hardwood." She reached down to pat Savannah, "I am not sure about her though. She may not like it but I think I could get some area rugs."

"All right then, you want a new floor and I want to use some power tools. Shall we find a store and see what we can find."

"What? Are you serious? This is not really what I had in mind. And what if the power goes off? I don't even know what I like and I have no idea how to put in a floor. I have never decorated anything in my life." She would have kept going on but she was out of breath.

"Relax," he said putting his hands on her shoulders. "I have installed plenty of floors. This is your house and your chance to do anything you want with it. It is totally your choice with no one to tell you otherwise." He cautiously slid one hand up her neck and ran his fingers through her hair. He wanted to slowly work in the idea of his coming back and this was part of his plan. "As far as losing power, whatever I don't finish I will come back."

Emma leaned back, eyes closed, into his hand. She knew it would come up eventually even though he definitely was scheming. She did not mind though, she found it sweet and flattering that he wanted to see her again. It no longer scared her to death; still a little cautious but for her it was progress. And hopeful that maybe she would not be alone forever. Maybe it would not be with him but she was gaining confidence that there was a possibility of true love out there for her.

She opened her eyes and with a smile said, "I am willing to go look."

Chapter 9

Two hours later they were back at the house stacking boxes of new engineered hardwood flooring in the garage. Emma surprised herself by choosing fairly quickly. She wanted something to last and something that would withstand the dog. She picked the engineered floor that could be refinished if needed. She picked a dark walnut that would hide dirt and hair.

The last box that came out of the van was a brand new table saw. Ben insisted on paying for it despite Emma's protests especially since he would be leaving it at her house. They carried it together and put it on the one table in the garage. Emma only had one basic set of tools and nothing with the word power attached to it. The previous owners of the house had left a workbench and some cabinets that were pretty bare right now. She was excited to learn some new skills though. It would be nice to be able to fix simple things on her own.

The rest of the evening was spent moving furniture, tearing up the carpet and padding and pulling up the tack strips. Emma cooked dinner while Ben swept then vacuumed the floor. It was pretty late when Emma put the last dishes away. Ben was starting to lay some of the new floor to see how it looked. He was also creating a starting point to make sure the planks would not end up crooked. Emma sat on the couch watching him in admiration. He was methodical, planned carefully and did not rush. Ben was very professional and she completely trusted that it would turn out nicely which made her realize something about the rest of the house. "You know what's going to happen right?"

Ben looked over suddenly broken from his focus, "what do you mean?"

"The new floor is creating a shiny new spot in my house. Now everything else will look really bad. The kitchen cabinets and vinyl floor all have to go now too. The bathroom needs updating, all the walls need painting."

Ben smiled at her, "sounds like I may need to come back a few more times."

Emma teased him, "I think I can figure out how to paint." But that was probably it she thought.

"Probably," Ben said thoughtfully, "but there are a lot of walls here and it would be faster with two of us."

"Well I can always hire some college boys to help me," she retorted with sinister glare.

"Fine," he shrugged and went about his business. Ben knew she was teasing him, or at least he hoped so. When he felt her arms wrap around him he definitely knew she was teasing. The hairs on the back of neck were standing from the little kisses she was spreading across his bare skin. He tried to focus on the planks but he was failing miserably. He was not sure how to take the gesture, was it a sign he could take things a step further? This was the first time she initiated this extent of physical contact. It was such a sweet and tender gesture that he so desperately wanted to pursue but he would not push his luck. He was almost glad when she backed off since he would not be able to resist her touch much longer.

Emma stepped back fairly abruptly. She knew Ben was showing great restraint and was thankful but she also felt bad. As she was watching him she could not help herself though. It was getting harder to ignore her own body's reaction. What started as a small awaking of feelings was turning into a full blown need for him.

The wind whipping outside her window redirected her attention. The rain was due to start in full force late into the night. It was a bit unnerving for her. She was glad she asked Ben to come and that he came up with something to keep them occupied. But now she was tired. She at least wanted to be lying in her bed. She stepped back to Ben and lightly put her hand on his back. "How much more do you plan on doing?"

"I just want to lay a few rows and that will make it easier tomorrow," he replied without turning back as he was fitting more planks together.

"I am going to lie down," she paused trying not to over think the situation. "Hey Ben?" He turned to look up at her. "I don't want to sleep by myself tonight, with the wind and the rain; I would just feel better if you were with me. I have Savannah with me but she's a pretty heavy sleeper and you know it is not quite the same. Okay, I am rambling, again. I am going now."

She turned but before she could get very far Ben grabbed her arm and pulled her back. He leaned in the rest of the way and kissed her softly on the lips. "I won't be long."

An hour later when Ben went to join Emma he found that she was still awake watching television. She was watching the weather channel. He had to admit it was fascinating to watch the progress of the storm with all the live reports. He was not so sure if Emma should be watching it though. She already seemed a little nervous.

As he was changing out of his work clothes he wished that she had fallen asleep. He would have been able to quietly climb into bed without disturbing her. It was going to be difficult being in the same bed with her while keeping his hormones under control. That is why he opted to sleep on the couch the night before. He looked at her with her eyes glued to the latest update, how could he decline such as sweet request to be kept company?

He assessed the situation; Emma was in the middle with Savannah on one side of her. He definitely would not try to move her guardian. He picked the other side and managed to keep a slight distance between them without feeling like he was going to fall off the bed. Emma immediately snuggled up against him. He gave into her warmth and let his mind relax. He felt so peaceful, calm and right. Right meaning this was where he was meant to be. This could in fact be the next stop on his journey.

He grabbed the remote and started flipping the channels. "I think you should take a break from this."

"Hey give me that," Emma said reaching across Ben but he kept it just out of reach. She shimmied on top of him pretending to make efforts to grab the remote. Instead of reaching out she held his head in both her hands rubbing his checks with her thumbs. She looked into his eyes and saw his desire for her but also sincerity. Emma felt ready to trust him with her emotions.

She leaned in and softly pressed her lips to his. Her body was sparking more than she knew was possible. "Make love to me, show me what it's like."

Ben rolled her off him and he propped himself up on one side so he could press part of his body weight on her without crushing her. He wanted nothing more than to make love to her but he wanted her to be sure. "I would love to but only if you are ready. I told you I will wait."

Emma pulled him down even closer to her. "I can't wait anymore. My body needs you and I want you," she told him pleading with her eyes. Her body had been on a slow kindling burn but now it was in full flames and she needed Ben to smother her smoldering body. While she did not fully know what to expect she was excited to find out.

Ben could no longer hold his emotions back either. The flood gates let open and a huge rush of desire filled every crevice of his body. He was in no rush though, he wanted to enjoy every moment, explore every part of her. He started with the familiar and took in her soft lips in full force. He moved down her neck stopping briefly at each new spot tasting and teasing at the same time.

He pulled her tank top off her and continued his exploration. His lips continued across her collarbone while his hand started slow circles around her breasts. By the time he closed in on her nipples they were hard and ready for more. As he moved down her body he let his hand trail across her navel before diverting to her hips.

Emma let out a whimper and raised her hips to his touch. She dug her fingers into his shoulder trying to urge him on. While she was enjoying the kisses and teasing she needed him to touch where the heart of the fire was burning the strongest.

Ben was enjoying her response to him and knew she was growing impatient and while he was not going to be rushed he would not torture her either. At least not too much he thought as he swirled past her hips and down her outer thighs and back up on the inside stopping just short of his final stop. After taking a final taste of her heaving breast he traced the outline left by his fingertips with his lips. When he reached the spot his finger left off he went back to where he started but let his fingers continue on. He continued his feast with her lips and tongue. Meanwhile his fingers were slowly dancing around moving in and out of the peaks and valleys. When she pulled her lips off his to catch her breath he pushed deep inside her causing her to let out another deep whimper. He went deeper as her hips rose in anticipation. His tongue and finger pushed and twirled and tasted and pleased in tandem. He followed the motion of her hips until he felt a tightening around his finger. He pulled out and danced a few more steps on her sensitive skin until she could not bear it any longer. Her body shook in relief as she pulled away from him.

Emma's fire had been super ignited and then dowsed until it became a small kindle. She was still hot and out of breath and every muscle in her body had melted into complete submission. Ben could do whatever he wanted to her at this point, she would not care. In her state of euphoria she did note that he rolled off the bed for a moment and she realized he had his own fire so Emma wrapped her arms and legs around him as he climbed on top of her. Even though he had brought her to her peak and back she wanted Ben to have the same experience. She wrapped her legs tighter around him and raised her hips to let him in deeper. He responded by pushing deeper and harder. His rhythm was slow at first until he could no longer maintain control. Ben's motion became quicker and more intense until his body collapsed on top of her.

Normally he would roll away but with Emma he did not want to let go. Not wanting to crush her he did roll over and pulled her on top of him. She snuggled into him resting her head on his shoulder. Ben ran his hands through her hair and across her shoulders. Now more than ever he knew this was who he wanted to be with. She was opening up to him and trusting him. He was already thinking about his next trip back and how often he would be able to visit.

While Ben's mind was in planning mode Emma's mind was mostly blank. She was enjoying the moment. Instead of rolling over and going to sleep he kept paying attention to her in a sweet and tender way. She made sure to ingrain the moment in her memory.

Whether or not she stayed with Ben, this would be the moment that would be compared to all others.

Emma woke up the next morning alone, even Savannah had left. She knew her guest was still there as she could hear the sound of the saw cutting her new floor. As for Savannah, Emma was a little disturbed at the change of allegiance. But it was not the sound of the table saw that woke her it was the howling wind and torrential rain. She was surprised that she had slept so long but now as the rain was pelting her window she had no desire to stay in bed by herself.

Emma put her shorts and tank top on smiling with the memories of the night before. She walked to the kitchen and saw Ben, shirtless, laying more planks on the floor. He was almost finished with the living room. There was still the hallway and dining room and she was doubtful he would make it much further considering the weather. Emma watched silently for a few moments thinking that there probably was never a time that Ben did not look sexy. She still had no idea why he chose her.

When Ben stood up to cut another board he noticed Emma was watching him. She looked awfully cute with her tussled hair and barely there clothes. He walked over to her, leaned over, and let his lips linger on hers. He stayed long enough to give her a little taste. He pulled away before he would feel the need to drop everything and drag her back to the bedroom. Besides not wanting to drip sweat on her he wanted to keep working. He stepped back smiling. "Good morning, I hope I did not wake you."

Emma smiled back partly disappointed that he stepped away but it was a nice way to be greeted. The wind howled again and she stepped over to the window to see the tree branches bending with the continuous wind. "No, actually it was the wind and rain."

Ben laid a reassuring hand across her back. "The heavy rain and wind shouldn't last but a few more hours. It will be okay. I am just trying to get as much as I can done in case the power goes out."

Emma felt a little better but the sky was almost black and there was some debris flying through the air. She needed a distraction. "Well, then, I'd better cook us some breakfast." She shimmied past Ben and went to the refrigerator.

While she was cooking Emma could not help but turn the weather channel back on for an update. It seems Ben was right that they had a few more hours of heavy rain, wind and some thunderstorms. After that the eye would pass but the rain was lighter on the back side of the storm. The winds would keep blowing though and with the ground saturated they would still have to be wary of falling trees. She watched a clip of the water pounding the boardwalk not too far from where Allie was. She hoped her friend was tucked in a safe corner of the hotel. She thought of

Alex as well as the storm would be riding up the coast and turning towards New England. He would be safe at his mother's house but it was a large estate they would have to ready. After being upset at his sudden departure she knew that he made the right decision to go help his mother.

Thirty minutes later she put Savannah's food dish on the floor and two plates on the table. She had made a skillet of eggs, onions and potatoes with a side of toast, coffee and orange juice. It was more than she normally ate in the morning but if the power did go out she would rather fill up on a big hot breakfast.

Ben followed the scent of the homemade meal, pulled on his tee shirt and joined Emma at the table. Savannah followed and sat patiently waiting for the little morsel she knew would be tossed her way. He gave her a pat before sitting down. "Have you always had her?" Ben asked referring to her dog.

"No, I got her after I moved here."

"Really? I just figured since she seems older that you had her a while."

Emma thought back to the day she adopted Savannah. She remembered the look in her eyes. It was as if she was saying I know I am old but I'm still worthy. "I was out shopping one day and the pet store was having an adoption fair so I stopped in. I never had animals but it occurred to me that I was living by myself and it might be nice to have a dog. They had a bunch of young dogs jumping all over the place and then there was Savannah. I thought she barked at me when I walked by her but I was not sure. I kept walking around the store debating what to do. I watched her from a distance and she did not bark at anyone else so I went by again. She barked at me again. Apparently she picked me. So I took her home. She is older and a little slower but she sure is loyal."

"She is very wise, knows a great woman when she sees one." Ben gave the dog an all knowing grin as if they shared the same thoughts.

They finished in silence as Ben was devouring his food. He scraped every last bit off his plate and finished his juice in one long gulp.

Emma watched amused but she was glad he was enjoying the meal. "You forgot to save a piece for the dog," Emma told him with a very serious look.

Ben looked at both the ladies, both looking back at him with equal intensity. He made a quick move and grabbed a chunk of eggs off Emma's plate and dropped them in front of the lady in question. He was doubly rewarded with a nudge from one and a nod from the other. Normally he would sit longer and even do the dishes but a thunderstorm was moving closer and he wanted to get more done so he could start the dining room. He knew he would not finish but he did not want to leave her house a mess either. He grabbed his coffee cup and gave Emma quick kiss, "that was delicious. Thank you."

Emma chose to remain at the table. She was glued to her chair as the rain pounded harder and louder on her skylights. She jumped ever time the lightning flashed and thunder rolled. She should be used to the thunderstorms by now as the area had incredible storms that blew in and out but they were usually short lived. She decided that the weather channel in fact was not helping so she started flipping though the other channels but nothing held her interest. She got up and sat on her new floor to watch Ben as he worked. Savannah sat besides her placing her head on Emma's leg. Her hand automatically started rubbing her dog's head.

Ben was aware that he had company. After he finished popping the row of planks into place he took a momentary break and sat on the other side of Emma. "What do you think so far?"

"It looks great, you do fantastic work. I'll write a review for you," she added with a smile.

"It's only fair since I wrote one for you."

"You did?"

"Of course, everything else aside," he leaned in and kissed her, "your tours are first class."

"Thanks." She would have to check her website. She could be doing some updates or printing photos but there was no way she would be able to focus.

"I am going to cut the next planks, do you want to help?"

"No, I am good sitting here." She flinched again with another loud crack of lightening that flashed white light throughout the windows. She noted that Ben seemed to hesitate for a moment also but he headed to the garage anyway. He was gone for about two seconds when there was a loud boom and a crackle followed by a last flicker of the lights before they all went out. There was also a shattering noise that caused Emma to jump up. She went back to the kitchen. She was not really sure why but it seemed a little safer there.

She was wondering what was taking Ben so long to come back in the house. She was getting antsy; she had no idea what she was going to do with herself. She breathed a sigh of relief when Ben finally emerged.

"Sorry about that, a branch hit one of the window panels on your garage door and cracked it. I put duct tape over it to keep the water from blowing in." As Ben was talking he threw off his shirt as he was covered in sweat and sawdust.

Emma was only half listening as she watched him take his shirt off. That was definitely a distraction. She remembered the first day they met and how he took his shirt off while they were kayaking. She took notice then and this was no different. She walked over to him, grabbed a dry towel and started softly drying the water off his damp back. She went across his shoulders and down his back. He stood quietly as she moved around to his front and up his chest. She dropped the towel but continued to tease him with her fingers while her lips softly kissed his shoulders. She let one hand travel south to check the status of his arousal. Of course she knew the answer already as his breathing deepened with every kiss and touch.

Ben thought he was warm from working but now his whole being was heated. He was enjoying the attention and held still while Emma explored his body but he would only be able to take it for a few more minutes before he would need to tear off her clothes.

They were both immersed in the physical emotions running through their bodies that they barely noticed the continued howling winds. But when lightning cracked with an immediate rolling of thunder Emma jumped, trance broken. Ben finally turned around and wrapped her in a protective hug.

Wanting to bring her attention back to where they were he scooped her up and carried her to the bedroom. It did not take long to rekindle their fire. Not only did they keep each other distracted, they kept each other occupied for the remainder of the heavy thunderstorms. Just as the intensity of the storm ebbed and flowed so did their emotions as they teased, tested and discovered what made them smolder. After they perfected their timing their intensity peaked and melted as one collapsing into each other's arms.

When the rains simmered down to a heavy drizzle and they exhausted their bodies, Emma perched herself so she could look into Ben's eyes. She was in a dream-like state. While she was ready for the storm to blow away she was not ready for the reality of Ben going back home. "So would making love to you always be like this?" she asked thinking she would always have something to look forward to.

"That would be my goal," he responded rubbing his hand though her hair. With Emma he thought it would be easy. He was attracted to her whole being physically and emotionally. He felt he was going to suffer from withdrawals which meant he did not plan to spend too much time away. "Looks like I will need to come back."

Emma sat up wrapping the sheet around her. She had such mixed emotions. "This week has been amazing and magical. You have brought out feelings in me that I have never even experienced. I'm worried that when you are not here I won't be able to hold on to those feelings. Ultimately I am scared of doing something that will break your heart because I don't know how to do this. I don't know how to handle a proper relationship let alone a long distance one. I certainly don't know how to handle these new sensations and emotions you have brought out." Before she could continue Ben's lips were on her again. "Sorry, rambling again," Emma managed to say in between kisses.

"Don't worry, I won't give you a chance to forget about me. I'll call, text, Skype, whatever it takes and then before you know it I will be right back here in this spot." He waited for some kind of response but he did not get one. He took her head in both his hands and turned serious. "I want to make this work, I want to try and I will do whatever it takes. Will you do this with me? We will still take it slow if you want and we will see what happens."

Emma could not find words, she was still nervous but she had come this far. She nodded yes and wrapped herself around him.

Chapter 10

In the end the storm did not cause too much of a disruption. The power came back on that night and what flooding had occurred receded the next day. Tree limbs and debris were quickly swept up and set out for pick up. The tourists resumed their vacations and Emma was back in business.

Because Ben had spent two extra nights away he, too, had to play catch up with his own job. While he was working into the evenings Emma was back to delivering photos and spending time on her computer. They did find time to talk to each other but it was often in short bursts while they were in between calls or taking short breaks. Their conversations were also frequently interrupted by Ben's business associates or clients. Emma was still willing to make the relationship work but she still had her doubts.

Not only did she have that on her mind but Alex was leaving for school the upcoming weekend. She had not found another helper which was going to put more physical work on her. Allie was getting antsy too. She was doing well at her job but her sights were set on New York. As soon as summer season was over the resumes would be going out.

With the imminent departure of one of her roommates and the eventual departure of the other, Emma agreed to one last outing with her friends. Alex's college friends were in town and Ben was not due in until the next day.

They agreed to dinner and drinks at the same oceanfront restaurant they had met Katie and Molly at earlier in the summer. After the meal they moved to the bar area where the drinks continued to flow and the conversation was lively. Emma did notice that one of Alex's friends, Austin, was taking an interest in her. She was flattered and made a point to be polite back without being overly flirtatious. At least that was her goal but the more she drank the less she knew what she was really doing.

Trying to focus back on the conversation she heard Alex talking about Katie. "How do you do it Alex? You guys have met only once but yet you act like there is no one else out there for you. How do you stay so committed to someone you never get to see?"

"We talk a lot, share our secrets and desires. As far as the physical part, it's the anticipation that keeps us going. And when we do get together I will feel like I already know her and what she needs. It will be special," he added a little quietly before taking another swig of his beer.

"Such a romantic," his friends teased him.

Emma thought it was sweet, "I will toast to that." They clinked glasses and Emma finished off her last few drops. She was feeling light headed and as much as she did not want to leave she was the only one of the group that had to work the next morning. She stood up but held on to the table to help her balance. "Well I don't mean to be a party pooper but I need to get up early so I am going to call a cab."

Austin quickly stood up, "I have not had anything to drink, I will take you home."

"Oh, sure, I don't live far."

Austin held his hand on the small of Emma's back. She did not think much of it, she was a little wobbly and it was nice he was guiding her out. Once in the car she closed her eyes and put her head back. Luckily she had prepared for the next morning's tour already so she planned on crawling into bed as soon as she got home.

A few minutes later they pulled into her driveway. When she turned to face Austin to thank him for the ride he leaned in and kissed her. Not only was she shocked she was also slow to react. Because she did not pull back right away he took it as a sign and kissed her harder. Finally her brain caught up and she pulled back. She was not upset, she was flattered and let out a little smile. It gave her another shot of hope and confidence even though there was no sparks with him. "Thanks again for the ride."

"Can I call you?"

Emma was enjoying the attention but not liking having to disappoint him. "I don't think this is the right time for me but I am really flattered."

"Yeah, you are right; I'm going back to school. But I had to try right?"

"I had a nice time. Good night."

Emma walked up to her door while looking for her keys in her purse. She reached the steps but jumped back when she saw the large figure before her. After the glare of the head lights from Austin's truck faded the figure came into focus. Her heart skipped a beat when she saw Ben. He was not due to come until the next day. It had been hard when he left and worse when they could barely talk. Now she was ecstatic, him being there was the perfect end to her evening.

Ben, however, did not share the same feelings. He worked extra all week so he could get back a day early. It had been complete torture for him to leave. Even though he had only been away for four days, it was four days too many. This brought him back to what he just saw. His blood pressure was topping out. It had only been four days and Emma was already kissing someone else. He could not believe his eyes. He was absolutely devastated. He felt like his heart was being stomped on with each step she took toward him and then she dared to look happy to see him.

Emma raced up the steps to give Ben a big hug but stopped short when Ben crossed his arms across his chest.

"What the hell was that?" he dug into her right away.

"What do you mean?"

"Are you kidding me?" First he was angry but now he was boiling. "Who was that?"

"Oh, that's um," she stumbled, her memory blocked by the surprise of seeing Ben.

Ben glared at her. "That guy just kissed you and you don't know his name?" The situation was getting worse and worse.

"No, I do."

"So who the hell is he and why the hell were you kissing him?"

Emma wished her mind was not so fuzzy. He was getting this all wrong and nothing was going right. She pushed past him and tried to unlock her door but she was having trouble lining the key up.

She gave up and pushed the keys into Ben's hand. With all her concentration she tried to set things straight. "Austin is his name. He is a friend of Alex's. We all went out since they are taking Alex back to school tomorrow."

Ben took the hint and unlocked the door and followed Emma inside, if he had not been so tired he would have gotten back in his car and went right back home.

"So what now, you'll see him on the side?" he accused her with an edge of sarcasm.

"What?" Now Emma was getting angry. "Ben, he kissed me," she stated with a rising voice.

"Oh is that right, it seemed like you lingered there a little too long."

Maybe he was right but it was not her fault. Why couldn't he see that? Savannah was whining so she followed her to the back door and let her out. "I didn't do anything. This is not my fault."

"Exactly. You did not do anything, push him away, break off the kiss, nothing." And now he was supposed to trust her every time he went back to New York?

Emma was done trying to convince him otherwise. She did not like the way he was overreacting and she especially did not like his display of anger. She let Savannah back in and started for the bedroom. "I don't know what else to say but I have to be up early so I am going to bed." Savannah followed but gave out a little whimper as she turned to look back at Ben. She followed Emma but circled a few times in the hallway before taking her spot on the bed.

Ben watched her go. He was still angry but it was slowly dissipating and being replaced by sadness. He really thought Emma was the one he would spend his forever with. She was everything he wanted, except loyal. He threw a pillow and blanket on the couch and flopped down running his hands through his hair. It was going to be a long night by himself. Definitely not what he envisioned. He thought about their love-making during the storm but then his body was betraying him. He had to clear his mind; the images of her soft curves were clouding his judgment.

He also wished he could ignore his phone but it kept beeping insistently.

"Hello mom," she would still be up, it was three hours earlier on San Diego.

"Ben, what is wrong, I can tell something is wrong."

Was it mothers intuition, he wondered. Whatever it was he was not really up for talking about it. "I'm fine mom. Is everything all right by you?"

"Ben, my chimes are a mess, a tangled mess and they are getting worse."

He sighed. He was tired of hearing about her precious chimes but he also would not lie to his mother. "Emma and I are not going to work out, that's all. Listen, why don't you cut the strings, unravel them and retie them?"

He heard his mother gasp, "I would never do that. I am sorry about Emma, I was really hopeful. You and the chimes will find a way to sort life out. Remember I am here for you."

"Thanks mom." He was grateful for the short conversation. He thought about what his mother said but could not imagine sorting anything out with Emma. Maybe he would go back to his old ways. No attachments, no commitments and no heartbreak.

Emma woke up the next morning feeling like crap. It was not from the drinking but from the whole mess with Ben. She slept for a few hours thanks to the alcohol but tossed and turned the last few hours. First she was mad at Ben but now she was mad at herself. She had opened herself up to him only to so quickly be judged. She should just go back to being single, no more being told what to do.

As she got dressed she heard banging noises coming from the front of the house. Heading to the kitchen she found Ben making quick progress on the floor. She was glad but also agitated. "You know there are other people in this house trying to sleep," she commented with an edge to her voice. She was not sure what time Allie and Alex had returned but she was quite sure they would not want to be wakened.

Without looking at her, he responded gruffly, "I won't be much longer. Then I'll be out of your hair," he paused before adding, "for good."

Emma did not realize how much those two words actually upset her. "Why are you doing this?"

"I promised you a floor, I don't break my promises."

She walked around him to face him. "No?" She asked glaring at him. "You promised you would be patient and understanding with me."

Ben put his tool aside and glared back at her with equal intensity. "Anything but another guy. That is where I draw the line. I didn't think I would need to spell that out for you."

Emma balled her hands, she would have yelled back at him had her roommates not been sleeping. "I did not do anything," she said gritting her teeth.

"Exactly," was his only response before walking off.

The morning had been a real struggle for Emma. It was hard to keep a happy face for a group of tourists. She did all the usual things; introductions, wildlife spotting, water fights and taking photos. It was hard to keep images of Ben out of her mind. She just did not understand what his problem was. It did not matter anymore, he made it pretty clear that they were finished. Maybe she would try again someday but for now she had to figure out what she was going to do when her roommates left.

She was grateful that Ben's car was gone when she pulled in her driveway. Allie was still home though and there was no avoiding her. She was not interested in explaining what happened or hearing about the other fish in the sea. She grabbed her camera bag and cooler and decided to go in and get the conversation over with.

She found her friend at her usual place, by her computer, with a cup of coffee. She flopped down on the couch waiting for Allie to say something first. Surely she knew Ben had been there. The floor was finished, which was really nice. Maybe if she stomped all over Ben's floor she would feel better. Probably not though, especially if she scuffed it up.

Emma watched as Allie took a last swig of her coffee before sitting down next to her. She laid her head on her shoulder and closed her eyes. It was the first moment she had to breathe and really take in what happened. She realized there were warm tears running down her cheeks. She could not remember the last time she cried. "I don't know why what I did was so wrong that he hates me now."

"Austin told us he kissed you when he got back to the bar. I did not think Ben would react so strongly. But I think guys like Ben just want their egos stroked a little."

"What do you mean?" Emma asked sitting up while wiping her eyes.

"He probably just wanted to hear that Austin was an ass for kissing you, or that you pushed him off, anything to let him be assured that he is the only one."

"He must know that another guy could be attracted to me. How many women are always trailing after him?"

"True, but he has been there and done that and you haven't. So now Ben will worry you might flirt with anyone and let them kiss you and it's no big deal."

"That's not what happened, you know that."

"You weren't flirting? I know you were enjoying the attention."

Emma was started to feel defeated but she was still confused. "I was being polite. Or is that flirting? Anyway I told Austin the timing was bad." She looked at her friend, she knew Allie was trying to help but, "I feel like you are taking Ben's side."

Allie leaned over and hugged her friend. "I'm not, but Emma, men are a jealous and possessive breed. It's not generally a bad thing but something to keep in mind. Ben is a good man, you should call him."

"I don't know, he made it pretty clear we were done."

Emma's phone started ringing, she had a split second of excitement when she saw it was a New York number but then she realized it did not quite match Ben's. She did answer it though out of curiosity.

"Hello?"

"Can I speak to Emma?" A female voice asked. There was a bit of static so Emma raised the volume.

"Speaking."

"My name is Molly. I hope you remember me. I went on one of your tours then we met up for drinks."

"Sure, how are you?"

"I'm in a bind actually and I hoped you can help. I'm in Fiji right now and I just found out the photographer for my wedding reception backed out. Will you come to New York and be my photographer next Saturday?"

This got Emma's attention but she could not imagine why she would choose her. "Surely there are plenty of other photographers in New York, why would you pick me?"

"I love the spontaneity of your photos. I don't want a bunch of formal poses."

"Thanks but I have never done a wedding. I don't even have any special equipment."

"I don't want special equipment, just you and your camera. I know you can do this. It's all expenses paid, oh and bring Allie and of course Katie wants Alex to come also."

"I don't know what to say. I have to check my schedule for next weekend."

"Please say yes, we will compensate you for any loss of business. Please, I really want you to do this."

Emma knew this was a great opportunity for her, "okay, I will do it."

"Thank you, I am so relieved. I will set everything up and send you all the details. Any special requests?"

Emma could only think of one thing, "Can I bring my dog?"

"Absolutely."

Emma filled Allie in on their upcoming trip. "Do you think you can take off?"

"After working every crappy shift all summer long they will have to give it to me."

"Alex will be so excited." Emma was starting to feel a little better about life.

"You should call Ben and tell him."

"I don't think so. Besides it is really a working trip, I don't need any conflict."

Chapter 11

The trio plus Savannah had driven to New York in Emma's van. Emma drove most of the trip but let Alex take over when they were close to the city. There was no way she was going to try to navigate city streets and crazy drivers. She was nervous enough about the trip. Having spent most of her life in a small town Emma was not sure how she was going to feel surrounded by crowds of fast moving people, tall buildings and concrete. She also spent the last week researching wedding photography but the more she saw the more unsure she felt. She knew Molly hired her for her candid and natural shots but she wanted to make sure she had a good mix. She also wanted to capture some special moments of Molly and Jason as well. Ultimately there seemed to be no good way to plan and as long as Molly had faith in her abilities she would go with the moments as they arose.

Molly and Jason had spared no expense by putting them up in a luxury mid town hotel that not only took dogs but pampered them just as they did their two legged guests. Since Emma was going to be in and out over the next two days she signed Savannah up for play time, a massage and a spa bath. She would also get special meals delivered to their room.

Their room was no less luxurious. They were in a two room suite on an upper floor. Large windows in the living room area overlooked the sparkle of the city skyline. The decor was plush and rich in color. Alex agreed to take the pullout sofa so the ladies could have the bedroom. The beds were as soft as clouds and piled high with duvets and pillows. After driving for eight hours Emma was looking forward to burying herself in softness.

The friends also learned they had an expense account attached to their room but they did not want to take advantage. What they did decide on was room service breakfast. They ordered before going to sleep and as scheduled the food arrived on time the next morning. Emma and Allie came out in plush white robes to find an assortment of fruit, pastries, omelets, toast, potatoes, juice and coffee. Even Savannah had a special plate of steak.

While the group savored the bacon and eggs they ate in relative silence, each one contemplated the activities of the day. Alex was anticipating a long awaited reunion with Katie. She had planned a walking tour of some of the older original architecture of the city. Allie was taking note of all the happenings inside the hotel and was planning on visiting some of the other iconic hotels of the city. Emma was being picked up by Jason and Molly to go uptown to the place where Molly had proposed. She thought it was so romantic that Molly proposed. She did not think she would ever have the guts to do that. She was not sure she even wanted to be asked again. She thought briefly of Ben. He was here somewhere in this big city of millions of people. He had not tried to contact her so she did not try to contact him. Emma let the memory go, she had a job to do. Since she was leaving first, she hit the shower first.

An hour later Savannah had been taken out by the dog walkers and Emma was ready to go. She had several memory cards ready for her camera. One was for city pictures. She knew her time and opportunities would be limited but she planned on just taking random photos as she travelled around. She was glad she had locals to guide her through the maze of streets and subways. As they moved through the streets she took shots of the buildings, street signs, street vendors and anyone or anything that looked interesting, which was pretty much everything for Emma. A couple of times she had to be nudged along since they were on a time schedule.

When they made it onto the subway Emma took a few shots but then took a break and asked Molly about their wedding trip.

"Fiji was beautiful," Molly stated with a sparkle in her eye. "We had a bungalow over the water. We could dive off our deck and go snorkeling and then watch the sunset at night. We got around by kayak if we did not want to get wet."

"That's amazing." Emma thought back to her wish. "Someday I hope to set up my business right on the water."

"If you work for it and hold on to your wish, dreams can come true."

Emma would remember that when she went back home. "So how is it you got married on your honeymoon and are having your reception now?"

Jason replied first, "my mother absolutely would not allow us to skip a reception. She was not thrilled to have us get married on a beach so after many debates we compromised."

Molly jumped in, "I have a small family anyway and I am not big on large overdone parties. But it seems that my new in—laws know just about everyone in this town so there was no getting out of it. So I planned our beach ceremony and she got to plan the party."

"You let her plan your party?" Emma's asked incredulously. She would never let her mother do that for her.

"My mother has been hosting parties all her life and it gave her something to do."

"I gave her general directions, I trust her. Actually tonight will be the first time we see the whole thing put together. So I am excited."

When they reached their stop and made their way back to street level Emma noticed a dramatic change in the cityscape. There were no flashy lights, no rushing crowds of people and the buildings were not as tall. Molly explained this was a more residential area and was where she lived when she met Jason. She showed her the building where she still owned her condo and pointed out the restaurants they went to.

When they reached the entrance of the park Emma changed out her memory card. She told Jason and Molly to take a stroll and pretend she was not there. They strolled slowly hand in hand wandering the paths through the well tended gardens. Emma followed them taking photos at different angles switching from color to black and white and sepia. She knew they had reached the spot where Molly proposed when Jason twirled Molly around before kissing her passionately. It was a beautiful moment that Molly captured from a low point of view. Looking from the ground the greenery of the trees created a halo around the couple. It was as if the draping branches bonded them together cementing their love. And while the couple was lost in their own world of passion Emma was lost in her own world of capturing their emotions.

Emma was not surprised to find the suite at the hotel empty when she returned. Alex would be escorting Katie, the maid of honor, and they were to ride in the limo with the bridal couple. Allie would be arriving on her own and Emma was scheduled to be picked up by a car service so she could arrive before the guests. The affair was to be formal but not quite black tie. Emma wanted to be able to easily mingle with the guests without standing out yet she needed to be comfortable and unrestricted. She chose black flowing pants and a shimmering halter top in black and silver sequence.

The reception was in a downtown loft space on the top floor of a converted warehouse. There would also be access to the roof which overlooked the water. When Emma entered the room her world was transformed into a nighttime pixie dusted wonderland. The ceiling was the night sky, dark but shimmering with stars. There were white branches everywhere dripping in glittering Swarovski crystals. The only flowers were white roses gathered in small bunches placed in front of each table setting. She guessed there were enough table settings for several hundred people. A small table with only two settings sat in the front of the room. There was also a large dance floor and a stage set up for a live band. Emma looked around enjoying the peace for a moment. She knew that once the guests started to arrive she would be very busy.

Since the ceremony had already taken place there would be no cocktail hour, instead the party would go on longer into the night. Emma was taking a few photos when the first guests arrived. She turned to find they were actually the guests of honor escorted by a tall woman who was likely the groom's mother. The couple had their eyes closed as they entered the room and Emma focused her lens on them to capture the moment of surprise. Upon the reveal, Emma followed the couple as they slowly made their way through the room taking in all the little details. She captured the smiles spreading across their faces and the tender moment between the bride and her mother-in-law.

Molly took Jason's hand and led him to the dance floor. They twirled around the floor in big sweeping steps. Emma's strapless A-line gown trailed softly behind her. Her dress was understated elegance that shimmered softly under the lights. Jason complimented his bride without taking the spotlight. Emma could understand Molly's desire to have a dance with just her husband. It was a special moment in a magical room that was soon to be filled with the obligation to mingle with hundreds of guests, many of whom she likely did not know.

The trio left the room before the arrival of the first guests. As was tradition, they were to be announced after the room filled. Emma took a break, she did have her own place setting at a table off to the side. She replaced her batteries and checked the space on her memory card. She sat down and observed the guests as they trickled in the door. Emma did not feel it was the right time to take photos. While the women looked glamorous in their glittering ball gowns and the men fine in their dark suits there was stiffness to the atmosphere. Emma wanted to wait until the drinks started flowing and the ambiance was more relaxed. That would be the best time to capture the candid photos Molly was looking for.

As the party started and the bridal party was introduced, Emma began to wander the room. She kept a slight distance as she followed the couple from table to table. Many of the guests took formal pictures with the bride but Emma waited to capture the smiles and the laughter and sometimes an occasional look of forced politeness. Emma felt the bride needed a break from the never ending introductions but as she was about to interrupt there was a tap on her shoulder. Emma turned to find Allie standing next to her. She gave her friend a quick hug. Allie was wearing an emerald green floor length dress. It had a fitted bodice that showed off her curves before falling softly to the floor. Emma smiled at her, "you look beautiful."

Allie smiled back but a look of concern quickly returned. "Emma, don't freak out."

"What do you mean?"

Allie looked across the room and nodded, "Ben is here."

Emma followed her gaze and saw not only Ben but his date. She was the type of woman she expected him to be with. She was tall and slim with milky white skin and long flowing blond hair. She had perfect poise as introductions were made. A perfect smile went with glistening eyes. Emma zoomed in with her camera and took a few shots.

She felt a twinge of jealousy. Ben should have been by her side. But her feelings quickly gave way to anger. Anger for the way he left her and anger that he was there. She did not expect to run into him in this city of millions. She was still taking shots when Allie interrupted her thoughts.

"I think you took enough pictures of them," Allie said quietly.

Emma was not truly shocked he had found another date already. She wondered if it was a first date or if they been other places. How did he know her anyway? And how dare he look so happy with her. "That's the type of woman I imagined he would be with."

"You need to stop selling yourself short."

"Maybe I was just an experiment for him, you know; see how it is to be with a plain Jane."

"I will not listen to you talk like this."

Emma sighed, she knew Allie was right. "I need a break." She looked back at the bride who looked like she could use a break as well.

She made her way over to the groom and bride and tapped Jason on the shoulder. "May I borrow your beautiful bride for a few minutes? I would like to take some portrait pictures outside. Give us a few minutes and you can join us on the roof."

Jason leaned over and kissed Molly softly, "I will be out shortly."

Molly thanked Emma silently and followed her to the roof top access. Guests would be allowed to go up after the dinner service. There was a bar surrounded by lounge chairs, ottomans and tables. The same theme was continued except the trees were live and they were laced with twinkling lights. Emma went over to the railing and took in the sweeping views of the river and lit buildings in the distance.

When Molly joined Emma she kept looking out in the distance and said, "You look beautiful. You and Jason look really happy together. You are both very lucky."

"Thanks, this party is a little much for me though."

"It's only a few hours, and then you will have made everyone happy." She was still staring out across the water.

"Are you all right?" Molly asked walking over to her. "Jason will be out soon, I thought we were going to take some photos."

Emma returned to her job at hand. "I am sorry, I just got distracted for a moment. Why don't you just walk along the railing, no poses."

Molly did as she asked but she was more interested in what was going on with Emma.

"So what distracted you, or should I say who?"

From behind her lens, Emma responded, "I just saw someone I did not expect to see."

"Who was it?"

Emma debated on telling her, she knew that Molly only knew a small percentage of the guests. It would not change things either way. "Ben, he's an architect. I met him while he was on vacation."

Molly could not suppress a smile. "So you did hook up." When she saw the look of confusion on Emma's face she added, "when I found out he was going to Virginia I suggested he take your tour. I thought you might catch his eye."

"Well I did, but it did not work out."

"I'm sorry to hear that." Before she could probe any further, Jason arrived. Just like at the park earlier, Emma let them roam around following, capturing their love on their own terms. She spent a few minutes with them before they were called back to their guests.

Emma took a bathroom break before she returned to the reception. Guests were sitting down for dinner and so she took advantage of the moment to freshen up. When she entered the ladies room Ben's beautiful blond date was standing in front of the mirror. She turned and smiled graciously at Emma.

Emma smiled back, she was curious about this woman. "I'm sure you hear it all the time but you are very pretty."

"Thanks, I'm Kirsten, and it's always nice to hear."

"Emma," she knew this would sound lame but she had to ask anyway, "are you a model by any chance?"

"Yes, actually I am."

Of course, Emma thought. She reached into her purse and pulled out a business card. "I might have taken a few pictures of you, if you want I can send you some for your portfolio."

Kirsten took the card. "That's really nice of you."

Emma noticed she seemed a little confused by her card, "I also do nature kayak tours, that's my main business right now but I think I want to expand more into photography. If you are ever in Virginia I can set up a photo shoot."

"My date mentioned he went kayaking in Virginia recently. Maybe you know him?"

Emma made a mental note to make a separate business card for her photography. Even though she thought it was interesting that he mentioned it to her she did not want to end up in a discussion about their relationship with his date. "Maybe, but I get a lot of tourists from New York." Luckily that seemed to satisfy her.

Emma let Kirsten leave the ladies' room first. She planned to wait a few minutes in the hope that she and Ben would be back inside the large reception hall and she could avoid him. But of course the plan did not work. As Emma left Ben was coming out of the men's room. Emma did not see him coming but felt herself lurch forward when he bumped into her. She scrambled to keep her camera from hitting the wall. A strong hand grabbed her elbow and helped her upright again. She turned to face the man who simultaneously almost ruined her evening but then saved it by keeping her camera from smashing. "Thank you," she said but when she looked up to see Ben her chest tightened. She bit her lip and backed away.

"Emma?" Ben could not believe his eyes. He dropped her elbow and backed away just as she had. He looked at her in disbelief. Here was the woman who broke his heart. The woman who said she would not be interested in coming to the city, the woman who looked as beautiful as he remembered. His body was betraying his desire to still be mad at her. His racing mind was interrupted when Kirsten waved a hand in front of him.

"Ben, I asked if you two know each other."

"Oh sorry," he looked at his date. His date, he wondered what Emma was thinking. He knew Kirsten through mutual acquaintances. He asked her after his last trip to see Emma. He figured it would be easier to go to a wedding with a date instead of being eyeballed by the single women. He also was aware of Kirsten's interest in him and she quickly agreed to go with him. This was becoming a nightmare for him. There were two beautiful women standing in front of him. One who wanted him, or was it two, and one he wanted for a quick fix and one he wanted forever.

"Looks like it's a small world," Emma jumped in. "Yeah I remember Ben from my tour. Good to see you again." She was trying hard to get out of the situation for the both of them but Kirsten, not being aware of their history, was not making it easy.

"Hey Ben, Emma said she would hook me up with photos for my portfolio and even some work where she lives."

Ben looked from one woman to the other feeling a little sick to his stomach. "Do you two know each other?" he asked tentatively, he was not sure he wanted to know the answer.

"Oh no," Kirsten answered cheerfully, "we met in the restroom, she mentioned she had taken some photos of me and that I might want them."

Emma blushed slightly. What the hell had she been thinking? And what was Ben thinking now?

The door opened and a blast of dance music echoed into the hallway. Kirsten jumped up, "oh Ben I want to dance."

"Go ahead, I will be right there," he grabbed Emma by the shoulder hoping to get a private moment with her.

Emma was irritated by the gesture, she really had nothing left to say to him. "I have to get back inside, there's a party going on I have to capture," she held her camera up.

"How come you did not tell me you were coming?" he asked with his own edge to his tone.

"You made it pretty clear that you did not want to see me anymore," she replied back with raised eyebrows. When he did not respond she added, "and I am here for just a short time." Still no response. "And I am working." Still nothing. "And what were the chances of us running into each other, I did not even know until just an hour ago that it was Molly who recommended my tour to you. You seemed to have left that out," she added a little more softly. "Well I have to get back inside, the party is heating up." She turned away quickly not wanting to give him another chance to grab her again.

She went back inside to a sea of people jumping in time to the music, hands raised in the air. She smiled when she saw Allie surrounded by good looking guys, finally letting loose and having some fun. Alex had a possessive hand around Katie while looking at her as if there were no other women in the room. Even Molly looked like she was starting to enjoy herself in this mass of party goers. The only thing Emma could do was to immerse herself back into the party, avoid Ben, not think of him and get back to the hotel then back home. She wiped a lone tear from her eye and jumped into the crowd.

Ben could not believe he had frozen. It was a first for him. He understood everything Emma said but surely she could have told him and set a few minutes aside for him. But then she was right that he did not give her any indication that he would see her again. The only way he could see out of this was to grab a few beers and fuzz out the memory. He went inside and headed to the bar.

Chapter 12

The newlywed couple was hosting a private brunch the next morning for the three out of town guests. They would also be previewing all the photos that Emma took throughout the day. The party had gone on well into the night. After the band had finished playing and a large portion of the guests had gone home, the party moved to the rooftop. It was a more intimate gathering and a more relaxed atmosphere. Even Emma managed to put her camera down for a few minutes to enjoy some moments with her new friends. Ben had already left which allowed Emma to relax for the last part of the evening.

Emma was tired but looking forward to the brunch. Besides having been out late, she had not slept well. Images of Ben had flashed through her mind all night long. They were the images that made her long for his touch again. But her reality kicked in when she remembered who he brought as his date. She set her feelings aside and got ready for the day. She was looking forward to seeing her work. After uploading the memory card to the computer Jason would hook it up to the big screen TV to watch the slide show. Emma had promised she would not preview or edit anything on the card. Molly wanted to see everything for better or worse.

When the trio made it to Molly and Jason's house they were feeling refreshed and excited for the day. Allie had been quiet about her plans but Emma was pretty sure she was sending out more resumes. Alex had another day of sightseeing planned with Katie. Emma had nothing in particular in mind but she had her camera and a fresh memory card.

Molly and Jason's loft apartment was a work in progress. Emma looked around at the high ceilings and the tall windows. There was the usual exposed brick on some of the walls but there was a general air of inviting warmth. The furnishings were light, big and comfortable which managed to blend well with the tropical flair.

It was the kitchen and outdoor patio that were still under construction. "I would have cooked for everyone but obviously I have no stove or countertops." Molly made a point to look directly at Emma when she explained the situation. Not that anyone minded. There was a delicious spread of every type of breakfast food from eggs and pancakes, to waffles and fruit and pastries. "And that's your fault," Molly told Emma half heartedly.

Emma frowned at the comment, this was the first time she stepped foot in the apartment or even this city. "How is this my fault?"

"Ben was supposed to have this finished by the time we came back. Now I know he's brooding for you and now it's interfering with his work."

"Oh, no, I am not taking the blame for this. If he weren't so thick headed we might still be together," she ended quietly.

"What about you? No stubbornness there?"

Emma turned her attention back to filling her plate. She did not go there to be criticized. "Ben left without saying anything and he had nothing to say last night. So can we just let it go?"

"For now," Molly conceded but she was not going to give up.

"If everyone will come to the table I can run the slide show while we eat," Jason announced.

Emma was not sure if it was good timing or Jason sensed a slight rise in tension. Either way she was glad to change the subject. She took a seat next to Allie.

Allie squeezed her arm and whispered in her ear, "remember she just got married, she's just rooting for love right now."

Emma smiled and relaxed. She dug into her breakfast and turned her attention to the screen. There was silence as the love of the couple played out amongst the beautiful backdrop of the park. Emma looked around. Everyone's eyes were glued to her work. They were mesmerized by what she created. She had initially been worried about the large number of shots she took but it actually gave the show a video like flow.

The scene shifted to the reception hall and as the tone of the photos lightened the chatter around the breakfast table picked up. Since Jason knew more of the guests he did most of the talking. They laughed, smiled, moaned and applauded as the night replayed itself. When the night played itself out Molly walked over to Emma and gave her a big hug. "That was truly beautiful, exactly what I wanted. I don't think anyone could have done that better than you."

Emma doubted that but she happily accepted the compliment. She was already picking out what would work best for her portfolio. Despite the distraction of Ben, she did have a good time and would consider adding wedding photographer to her resume. Her thoughts were disrupted when she noticed Molly scrolling back. Emma pretended to focus on finishing her fruit when she noticed Ben's date frozen on the screen.

"Do I sense a bit of jealously here?"

"Well she is pretty," Katie commented on what Emma was thinking and Alex gave her a look of disbelief. "What? Any photographer would have zeroed in on her."

"She actually is a model. And she seems pretty nice. Why wouldn't he want to be with her?"

"He was watching you most of the night, I don't think he even danced with her," Molly said.

Then Jason added, "if he really wanted to be with her, he would not have let her go two inches away from him."

"Maybe, but she sure did not seem interested in anyone else."

"That's because Allie had all the single guys occupied," Alex teased her.

"What, I'm not allowed to have fun?"

"Of course, I just was not sure you knew how."

Allie kicked her brother under the table and gave him a smirk. She was not mad at him though. She had chosen not to date for a reason. She did not want to be distracted on her path to land a job in this city.

"Anyway, you should go see him," Molly said to Emma to get the conversation back on track.

"I don't know." Emma felt herself waver. She did miss him but she did not know what good it would do. "I feel like I would just be setting myself up for more heartbreak. Besides, why should I make the move, he could have talked to me last night."

"He is thick headed but I know he will come around if you give him a chance."

"I was thick headed, it took me months to straighten myself out, I was just lucky she was still available. Don't risk losing a good thing." Jason leaned over and gave Molly a soft kiss to seal what he just said.

"What would I say to him?" She already tried, she did not know what else would convince him.

"Just tell him how he makes you feel."

"And tell him to get back to work."

"You have his address right? If not, I think I have it somewhere."

"It's ok, I have it on my phone."

"Hey Emma," Allie had a plan, "I have an appointment not too far away. I'll take you to his building then I am certain he can make sure you get back to the hotel. Later on," she added with a wink and a smile.

"Why I am the only one not feeling so confident about this? What if he's not home? What if he has nothing to say to me?"

"There's only one way to find out." Molly walked over and gave her new friend a hug. "Emma, Ben just needs a little nudge. He'll come around, I'm sure of it."

Thirty minutes later Emma and Allie were standing outside Ben's building. It was on a quiet, tree lined side street. All the buildings appeared to be residential but it was a quick walk to the subway and shops. Allie had managed to get them on the right subway train and out just a few blocks away. Emma noted that she had been studying the maps. Another sign of her desire to live there. Emma would not have been brave enough to try that on her own. She already noted that there were cabs going by frequently. She figured she would need one to get back to the hotel.

She milled around outside. She still had no idea what to say. She wanted to believe Molly but she always carried doubt with her. He had made a lot of effort to erase that doubt so maybe she needed to do the same for him.

"Come on, time to go in." Allie grabbed her hand and dragged her through the door. She led her to the security desk and signed her in. "I have to go, you'll be fine. I'll see you later tonight." The two friends hugged and parted ways.

Emma had no choice but to go to the elevator. It would look suspicious if she hung around the lobby and it would just be wasting time. She needed to get this over with. By the time the elevator came there were several other people waiting. Emma gave the appropriate nod and smile to the others as they got on. Emma got off on the fourth floor which was a middle floor. She had to squeeze through the others which meant she could not see beyond the doors.

She inevitable bumped into the person waiting on the other side. "Oh, I'm sorry." She looked up at the tall blond. Her chest squeezed tight when she realized she knew who it was. What would the chances that Kirsten lived on the same floor in the same building as Ben? Her heart sank even further when she realized she was wearing the same dress from the wedding.

Kirsten had been searching through her purse. She finally looked up. "Oh hi," she took a moment then realized, "you're the photographer from last night."

Emma wished there was an escape route. She didn't even see a stairwell nearby. She was pretty sure she had her answer about Ben. It seemed he made his choice. She would wait for his new girlfriend to get on the elevator then she would take the next one. She was sad but at least she had her answer.

"Hey Kirsten," a male voice said somewhat out of breath. Ben had found Kirsten's phone just after she left. He really wanted to catch her. He raced down the hall hoping the elevator was being its usual slow self. When he turned the corner he stopped short. This could not be happening again. Emma and Kirsten in the same space, at the same time. While he was freaked out he quickly vowed not to freeze like he had the night before. He was going to talk to Emma. He thought this would be his last chance to figure her out.

"You forgot your phone," he handed the forgotten item to his date but quickly turned his focus to Emma.

Emma had to focus to control her breathing. She wished she could look away but he was standing there in just his shorts. She wanted to reach out and touch him one more time but then the thought that Kirsten had probably just done that made her sick. Where were the stairs? She bit her lip fighting back a tear. She felt so trapped with no way out.

The elevator came and Kirsten gave Ben a kiss on the cheek and a hug. "Thanks, see you later," she said with a smile. "Don't forget my photos," she waved to Emma.

Emma forced a smile. "I won't." She watched the elevator doors close, gathered quick courage and looked at Ben. "I shouldn't have come here." She looked away and reached for the down button but before she hit it Ben's hand pulled hers away.

"You are not going anywhere." He tugged on her hand in an attempt to bring her back to his apartment.

"Stop Ben," she pulled hard and freed her hand. She pushed the down button repeatedly. "You made your choice. It's okay, just let me go."

"I will not." But he knew she would not go with him willingly. In one swift move he spun her around and threw her over his shoulder.

Before she knew what happened, Emma was facing the floor. "Put me down," she yelled at him pounding on his back. But that only resulted in him tightening his grasp. When he did put her down she was sitting on a soft leather sofa in his living room.

She looked around briefly and noted the dark furnishings she expected of a single man but liked the contrast with the cream walls. She wanted to get up and look at the photos on his bookshelf, see what was in his refrigerator, count the number of pillows on his bed. She balled her hands, the bed that Kirsten had just left. Why had he dragged her back here? "So did you make love to her, Ben? Or was it just sex this time?" Emma glared at him.

Ben crossed his arms over his chest. He deserved that. "You of all people should not make assumptions."

Emma's phone was ringing, she pulled it out of her purse while she responded, "But she spent the night here." She looked at the number and ignored the call. "And don't talk to me about being judgmental. At least I did not invite Austin to spend the night with me."

He grabbed a sweatshirt from his coat rack and threw it on. It obviously would not help to be standing half naked trying to convince her that nothing happened. He sat down on the club chair next to her and rubbed his hands through his hair. "Nothing happened."

"Was that your choice or hers?" Her phone rang again, same number as before, she continued to ignore it.

"You caught me off guard last night. I was upset, hurt and angry. You are right; I brought Kirsten back here to sleep with her. But I couldn't. I kept thinking of you, picturing you."

"So what do you want me to say? You gave up on me for a kiss I did not initiate and now I'm supposed to say all is okay because you did not sleep with your date?" Emma was startled by her very persistent phone. But then she needed the break from this pointless conversation.

"What do you want Charlie?" she asked her brother harshly.

"Mom is going through with it this time."

Emma stood up and went over to the window. "She has said that before. Why is it different this time?"

"She's ready, she left the house and she wants you to come and get her."

Emma groaned. She had not planned to ever go back to her hometown. At least not this soon. "Can we meet in the middle? I'm already in New York. Maybe you can bring her to somewhere in Massachusetts, and I will get her from there."

"You know I can't be involved in this."

"Damn it Charlie, this is our mother." Emma wanted to scream at her brother but she did not want Ben to overhear.

"I'm sorry, I have too much invested here."

"I left," she said more loudly out of pure frustration. Then she remembered where she was. "I'm surviving." She added more softly.

"I'm sorry. I just can't."

"Fine, I'll figure it out. Where is she?"

"At Anne's house."

"Okay, but it's going to be a few hours. She'd better be ready because I'm not hanging around." She hung up the phone without waiting for a response.

Ben had been watching Emma. He could not hear her but he could tell she was upset. Nothing about this morning was going right. He walked over to her and ran his hands through her hair, "tell me why you came here."

Emma missed his touch. She did not want to be mad anymore. She still wasn't sure if they could fix this but for now she had other problems to deal with. She turned to face him. She actually let a little grin slip, "Molly told me to tell you to get back to work and finish her kitchen."

Ben was relieved to feel some of the tension dissipate between them. "I'll admit I slacked off this week."

Emma had no time for useless chatter, she needed help. She thought about all the events of the past two days that landed her in this place at this point in time. She needed Ben right now and somehow he was with her. He always seemed to be there for her when she needed help. "I need a big favor."

"Of course, anything." His heart leapt, he really would do anything for her. He knew it was a lot for her to ask, he would do whatever he could.

"Hear me out before you say yes." She really wanted him to go with her but did not want him to feel any obligation.

He looked at her a little quizzically, "what is it?"

"I need to go to my hometown, in New Hampshire and fetch my mom. She's ready to leave my father and I need to go get her tonight."

His face turned to concern, "is she okay?"

Emma shrugged her shoulders, "she will be. I just really don't want to go by myself. I never had any intention of going back there and," she hesitated, "I'm just a little nervous."

Now Ben looked confused along with worry. He remembered back to when Allie had told him not to dig too much into her past but now he needed to know. "Tell me why you left."

Emma knew she would have to tell him eventually, he deserved to know. She picked up Ben's hands in hers. She missed his hands, they were strong yet soft and warm. She looked out the window again before answering, contemplating how much to tell him. She really did not have time to tell him everything. Nor did she want to relive it all. The whole point of moving was to get on with her life. "Justin became very controlling over time and I did not see it until the end. He started hitting me." She felt Ben's hands clench down on hers. She brought them to her lips and gave them a soft kiss to ease his grasp. "Eventually I fought back. I won the battle but I lost the war so I left." She let his hands go and made a motion to gather her purse.

Ben was battling to control his anger. Men like that had no right to be walking free in his opinion. He hoped he never crossed paths with her ex. He took a few deep breaths to calm himself. At least now he understood her hesitancy to trust and be in another relationship. "I wish you would have told me sooner." He really did, they may not have ended up in this mess if she had. Even though they seemed to be headed back to trusting each other he knew they both still had some making up to do.

He was right Emma thought to herself but, "I did not want to be judged," she finished simply.

Ben grumbled slightly at that. "I would not have judged you, who would do that?"

"You would be surprised." But that was all she was willing to say at the moment. "So will you come with me?"

"Of course," there was no way he would let her go alone knowing what he knew now. "Do you think Justin will be there?"

"I have no idea. I hope to grab my mom and turn right around and come back. And right now I'm exhausted so I will need you to drive."

"No problem. Give me a minute to change."

"We will pick up the van at the hotel and I want to bring Savannah as well."

She called Allie and Alex while she waited for Ben to get ready. She did not have a good feeling about this but at least she would not be alone.

Chapter 13

Ben looked in the rear view mirror. Emma was passed out asleep with her head on a pillow leaning against the side of the van. He wanted to talk some more, find out what was happening with her mother, what went wrong with her last relationship, who were her friends, where she learned to kayak. He wanted to know everything. He whispered all these questions to Savannah, who was sitting in the front seat next to him, but she would just cock her head at him. He reached over and patted her on the head. She was a great companion for Emma and seemed to have some insight into life that most people did not.

The busy roads of Connecticut eventually turned to quiet forested hills of Massachusetts. At some points there was almost no radio reception and he tried once again to talk to Savannah but even her eyes were starting to close. When they reached civilization again Ben noticed his phone coming alive with a string of missed calls and text messages. He planned to pull off at the next rest area so he could stretch real quickly and check his messages. Whatever it was though, would have to wait.

Finally he came to a rest stop and he pulled into a parking spot and climbed in the back. He gently shook Emma until she stirred. "Hey, just taking a quick rest stop break. I did not want you to wake up to see me gone."

Emma stretched her whole body out and then her head and neck. Sleep came quickly but not quietly. She had a lot of images flashing of her mother and father and Justin. With any luck they would be right back in this spot on their way home in a few hours. She looked out the window. "Where are we?" she asked groggily.

"We are close to the New Hampshire border. Why don't you get out and stretch your legs?"

Emma nodded in agreement. It would be good to get out and shake off some of her nerves. She leashed up Savannah and headed outside. All three took turns using the restroom. Emma took Savannah back to the van while she waited for Ben. She took the front passenger seat this time with only a small grumble from her dog. She settled on the center of the second row so she could see both her companions and out the front window.

Emma watched as Ben came back towards the van texting away on his phone. When he got back in he tossed his phone aside as if he was annoyed with the phone itself and not the messages it transmitted. "Everything okay?"

"Its fine," he said with a small laugh. "It's just my mother and her prophecies again."

Emma grimaced slightly. "I don't want to know."

"Good, besides it's a bunch of crap anyway." He gave his mother a brief update but she insisted that the original warning of love, friendship, betrayal and danger were still all true. It really did not matter to him anyway. He would take whatever was to come at this point. And he would not let his jealously and anger get in the way this time.

They continued on in a somewhat uneasy silence. Ben wanted to ask all the questions he thought of earlier but he did not know where to start. He also did not know if this was really a good time for that. He hoped they could get to the point where he could ask her something without even considering if it would make her uneasy. He wanted her to be able to tell him anything.

Emma stared out the side window in silence. A part of her wanted to tell him everything but she was mentally burnt out from the whole weekend. If he stuck it out with her through this trip she would definitely be more open with him, assuming it was not too late.

When they crossed into New Hampshire Ben finally broke the silence. "It's quite beautiful here. A lot different from San Diego."

"Yeah, especially in the White Mountains."

"And you don't want to go back?"

She shrugged her shoulders, "I think there's enough to do in the south to keep me busy. I do have some good memories here but the country is big and there is a lot more to see. After the summer season I think I will take Savannah up to the Blue Ridge Mountains for some hiking."

"You should, you deserve a break." Of course he wished she had included him in her plans. Actually he preferred if she did not go hiking alone but he was not going to say anything. As a matter fact she was probably more capable of surviving in the wilderness than he was.

"The exit is coming up," Emma said pointing to the sign. "It's only another forty five minutes from here." Emma directed him off the highway and through country roads until they reached a small picturesque town. They wove through town and then to the outskirts with tree lined streets with clapboard-sided houses. As they moved away from town the houses became more spread out and eventually gave way to farmland. They pulled onto a nondescript driveway and bounced down the gravel towards an old farmhouse.

Ben stopped the van a small distance from the house but did not get out right away. He was waiting for a cue from Emma. He looked at the house and noticed that the house itself and surrounding gardens were clean and simple and well kept. The house was old with multiple chimneys and a classic front porch, complete with a swing. It definitely needed a lot work but he could tell it was loved. It was the type of house he would love to get his hands on for a complete restoration type project. Someday, he thought to himself, but for now felt they needed to go in and get out. He reached over and squeezed Emma's hand. "Ready?"

"No. I just hope there is no one else there."

Ben was not exactly sure why she was so nervous. He knew she kept in touch with her mother and that her mom asked Emma to come. There was no point in sitting around. He unlocked the doors, "come on let's get this over with."

They walked up to the old farmhouse and Emma knocked on the door. After a few minutes the old door creaked open a fraction. A woman peaked out the door and after confirming she knew who was there she swung the door open and grabbed Emma in a full hug.

"Oh honey, I am so glad you came. Charlie told me you were in New York and I just knew I had to do it this time." She started shaking and the tears were flowing.

Emma followed her mother into the house with Ben and Savannah trailing behind. After pulling away from her grip she faced her mother to take a good look at her. Other than the makeup streaking down her face, she looked her usual put together self. Her father had always wanted her ready to greet any important person at any given time. She brushed her hair away from her wet eyes. She also wanted to check for any more incidents of clumsiness her mother claimed to have.

When she did not see anything she said, "It's going to be okay mom. He did not hurt you did he?"

"No, not physically," she sat down on an old floral couch in the living room. That would be the closest she had come to admitting that he had in the past. "I have felt so trapped since you left. I have nothing to do except to continue to cater to him. I asked if I could take some art classes and he just laughed at me saying I had no talent. I tried to join a book club but he always managed to plan a dinner on the same night. I can't even plant my own flowers since he hired the landscapers. I can't take it anymore, I'm bored and lonely. I'm scared too. What if he comes after me?"

Emma sat down next to her mother. She completely understood. "We'll get a restraining order if you want. I don't think he will though. He'll just spin some story that you are crazy. Just like he did for me."

"What am I going to do though?"

"Well for starters, you will stay with me. Then we will figure it out. There are lots of things you can do. You have planned some amazing events over the years. You were president of every PTA that I can remember and you were head of the winter snow festival."

"He said the festival was getting boring and I needed to step down." The tears started flowing again. "I didn't believe him at first but no one protested."

"You know people are scared to go against him. Everyone loved the festival last year."

Ben stood in the foyer watching the two women, his heart breaking for both of them. More so for Emma's mother. At least Emma was able to get out of her relationship. No woman deserved to be treated like they had been. He was glad they had not run into any trouble so far. The longer they were there the higher the chance they would. While he did not want to interrupt the reunion he felt like they needed to get back on the road. He stepped into the living room.

"He did not believe me when I said I was leaving. He said I did not have the guts. First he laughed but then he got angry. He said I better be there when he came home. He came towards me but luckily Bill was at the door. It's game day at the bar. He growled when he left and said he would deal with me later. I couldn't think, I couldn't move, I was so scared. I managed to call Anne and she came and got me."

"Where is she now?" Emma asked.

"She has to work an overnight shift at the hospital."

Emma looked up to see that Ben had come into the living room. He looked distressed. She knew it was hard being thrown into this situation. He nodded towards the door and she nodded back in understanding.

"Mom this is my friend Ben, he's going to drive us back to New York. We really should get going."

Her mother looked up in somewhat surprise. She had not realized another person was in the house. "I'm Grace, I appreciate you coming." She wiped her eyes and pushed back her short hair. She was on automatic pilot making sure she looked reasonable for her guests. She took a deep breath and gained her composure. "I need a favor before we leave."

Emma was afraid of this, if they delayed, her mother might change her mind. "I don't know if we have time, we really should leave."

Her mother started to tremble slightly. "Please," she looked at Ben too, "I need a few things from the house. I wasn't thinking when I left everything behind. And if I go back I might not be brave enough to leave."

"I don't know if this is a good idea." That was the last place she wanted to be.

"Please," she said again, "he said he would burn everything if I was not there when he got home."

"And you don't think he will be back yet?"

"No it's too early still."

Emma grimaced, this was not a part of her plan. She looked at Ben, hoping for an answer from him. He gave her a slight nod. "Okay, but I'm only grabbing a few things then we are getting out of here. And I'm leaving Savannah here with you."

A few minutes later they were back in the van. Emma had her mother's key to her childhood house and the new security code to get in. She was very anxious for this to be over with. The house was only ten minutes down the road. She figured ten minutes there, ten minutes inside and then another ten back and they would be heading home. She understood why her mother asked her to do this. There were a lot of years of memories in that house for good or bad and it was all her mother had and knew.

Emma debated on parking in the driveway or on the street out of view. She ultimately decided the driveway would allow them to get in and out of the house faster. They did drive past the house though and when they did not see anything unusual they pulled in the driveway.

The house was a sprawling brick ranch with perfectly manicured lawn and flower beds lining the driveway and sidewalk. Every window had matching country curtains perfectly tied back and the door had a matching floral wreath.

Emma had instructed Ben on the location of the photo albums her mother requested. While he did that she was going to get her mother's jewelry box and take a quick scan for anything else. They planned on taking no more than three fast trips in and out and they would be on their way. She was so nervous she was close to tears. But she had to do this, for her mother and for herself. She would not let her father win.

Ben turned off the engine and looked over at Emma. She looked like she was going to break down. He reached over and brushed his hand through her hair. He had a slight bit of nerves himself but he would not let anything happen to her. He leaned over and gave a soft kiss of encouragement. He missed her sweet taste and immediately wanted more but he knew their time was short. He forced himself to pull back. "Are you ready?"

The kiss was the shot of confidence she needed. She promised herself another one once they were on their way back. She managed an unsure smile and she nodded. She gave Ben the key and code since she did not trust her hands wouldn't be shaky. She was worried she would mess it up setting off the intruder alarm.

Ben took a quick second to adjust the key and took one last look at the code. He unlocked the door and held his breath as he entered the numbers on the panel. It did cross his mind that it may have been changed. When there was no alarm he let out his breath.

Emma sighed in relief also. She squeezed Ben's shoulder in appreciation and walked past him into the living room. She pushed back the wave of emotions that hit her by being inside her childhood home once again. As she headed to her parents' bedroom she felt a bit of sadness for feeling like she will never have a home to go back to. So many memories flashed through her mind at once. She felt like the scared and worried little girl she sometimes was. It was the memory of always needing to please her father and what would happen if she didn't, but then she was quickly comforted by the memory of the taste of her mother's fresh baked cookies and cakes. She remembered the sleepovers she had when her father was out of town but then she shuddered at the repercussions of the occasional bad grade. She squeezed her eyes shut and forced the memories away.

Out of habit she quietly opened the door and slipped inside her parents' bedroom. It was off limits to her as a child but like all kids she occasionally snuck in to look around. One time she got caught by her father. She shuddered at the tongue lashing she received. That was the last time she snuck in there. She shook her head clearing her mind. She grabbed her mother's jewelry boxes and headed back to the van. When she was back in she looked at the photos on the wall. There used to be photos of her from school and graduation. They had all been replaced. She made a mental note of it as she quickly made her way back to the bedroom and grabbed whatever was in her mother's night stand and carried that load outside. Ben was also putting another stack of photo albums in the back.

The pair made their way back in the house for the agreed upon final trip. Emma ran down the hallway and stopped at the door to her bedroom. She hesitated before opening it. When she did manage to look in she almost fell to the floor. It had been wiped clean as if she did not exist. The furniture and pictures were all gone. The walls were repainted and carpeting removed. She understood the need to update a kids room to a guest room or for some other function. However every trace of her existence was gone. Her father told her she would always have a place here but now it was like she had been wiped clean of the house.

She closed the door and went back to the living room. She was done, she was ready to leave. Her mother would have to replace whatever they did not get. She met Ben who was coming out of the kitchen with a few recipe books in his hands; they nodded to each other and headed back to the door.

Ben had left the key in the door so he could lock it more quickly. But he did not get the chance. When they went outside they were met by two squad cars and four sheriffs pointing their weapons at them.

Chapter 14

"Drop what is in your hands and put your hands up!" the sheriff yelled.

Ben dropped the cook books instantly and raised his hands. A wave of anxiety rushed over him. He had never been in this situation before. You can read about it and see it on television or in the movies but there was nothing like the feeling of having guns pointed at you. Then his mind started racing, this was a little excessive he thought. He looked over at Emma and was surprised to find her with her hands on her hips glaring at the officers.

"Sheriff Jones," she yelled, "we have permission to be here. We have a key and the code to the alarm."

The sheriff grinned evilly back at her, "Miss Emmaline Caroline you in fact do not have permission to be here. Your daddy changed the code just this evening. He had the one your mama gave you hooked to our silent alarm system to alert us of any intruders."

"We are not intruders."

"Miss Emmaline you forget who you are dealing with. Your daddy thinks of everything."

"I have permission to be here and you know that." Emma felt her anger rising, she did know who she was dealing with. Her father was playing games with her and she was going to lose again.

"Your mama chose to leave and that means she no longer has any rights to this house or its contents."

Emma slowly bent down to pick up the books, "and what is dear old daddy going to do with cookbooks Sheriff Jones?" She had to hold back from throwing one of the books as she feared it might make one of them jump and actually shoot at them. "She has lived here for thirty years; of course she still has a right to her belongings."

"Perhaps that should be left to the judge. So why don't you put the book back down and my deputies here will escort the two of you to the jail."

Jail? Ben thought to himself, he did not want to panic but he could not believe what was going on, he had to say something. "Sheriff," he called out to get his attention. "Surely there must be some misunderstanding, I think we can work this out if we just show you . . ."

The sheriff was not interested in what Ben had to say, he was just an unfortunate problem he would have to deal with. "You need to be quiet boy if you know what is good for you."

"I will put this down if you put it in the car for me, then you need to lock the door and have one of your boys bring the van to the station," Emma said.

Ben looked at her, "Emma I don't think we should be making demands."

Emma looked back with a serious look, "don't worry, they will do it. Give me the keys to the van."

Ben was worried about reaching into his pocket; he looked at the sheriff who gave a slight nod with his head. He slowly reached down with one hand keeping the other hand up. He noticed the deputies raising their weapons to the ready fire position. He slowly pulled the keys out of his pocket and jingled them so they would know it was in fact just keys. He dropped them on the ground and stepped back. He was relieved to see the guns being lowered as they approached. He took another glance at Emma, she still had not raised her arms but she was staying still glaring at the deputies. He was surprised at her calm and collected self. She had been so nervous around him but in this situation she seemed rock solid. He was feeling lost and confused and he needed to think fast on how to get out of this situation.

The deputies approached them; guns now holstered, and reached out for their arms. The deputies handcuffed them and escorted them to the car. They both went without resistance and without comment. They were placed in the same patrol car. Luckily they were handcuffed with hands in front so they could sit slightly more comfortably.

Ben, still in disbelief over what was happening looked over at Emma and quietly said, "Emmaline Caroline?"

Emma shrugged, "family names." She looked out the window. She knew the roads and knew the ride would be short. She knew Ben must be steaming inside but there was little she could do about it at the moment. There was not enough time to explain. It was unfortunate but she would have to wait and hope he could be understanding one more time.

"Don't worry about a thing, I will take care of this," Ben said interrupting her thoughts.

"It will be okay Ben, I am not worried."

"Well I am," he lashed back a little harshly. "I will find us a lawyer. I get to make a call right?" he asked the deputy.

"Sure, but I don't think you will need to do that," he replied while chewing on a toothpick. "Now you two need to be quiet back there. I don't want any conspiring going on," he added with a slow twang.

A few minutes later they pulled around to the back of a brick building. They were brought through a secure door and sat down on a bench in front of a high desk. They were followed in by the sheriff and a second deputy who had driven the van behind them. When Ben saw them he stood up to ask for a phone call but he was immediately pushed back down onto the bench. "I want to make a call. I need to get in touch with a lawyer," he said in a slow and clear voice.

The sheriff just laughed at him, "boy you don't need to call a lawyer."

Ben was frustrated, his hands were clamped together, and he needed to hit something. "I have a right to a lawyer," he said though clenched teeth.

Sheriff Jones grinned even bigger and looked at Emma, "he doesn't know does he?"

Emma stared back but did not respond.

"Know what?" Ben asked. He turned to Emma and said, "what is he talking about?"

"I'm a lawyer Ben," she replied quietly.

Ben was shocked. "You told me you worked with your dad but left out that little fact."

"I changed careers," she said nonchalantly.

Ben glared at her, he did not know what to say. He thought he knew her and was starting to understand her but now he was back to having no idea. He wondered what else she had not told him.

Emma felt the heat of Ben's anger. She needed to say something but she knew she would only have another minute to speak. "Listen to me, you need to trust me. We are only here because it is Sunday night and they will tell you they are not going to call the judge in. They have no case and they know it, they will let us go in the morning."

Before she could go on a female deputy came down the hall. She looked at Emma shaking her head, "I did not expect to see you back here. Come on, I'll take you back."

Emma stood up and looked back at Ben one last time. She was sad to see him in such a state of distress. She just hoped he knew her enough and would not make any harsh judgments about her. Emma followed her jailer. When she was locked in she called out hoping she could appeal to her as a woman. "Please call my mom and let her know what's going on."

The deputy nodded in understanding and walked away.

Ben watched her go. Every passing moment of this day brought more confusion. Surely she had been there in the capacity of a lawyer but he had a feeling there was more going on. He decided he needed a straight answer. "I take it she's been here other than as a lawyer."

"Come on," the sheriff directed, "we'll have a little talk on the way to your cell."

Something caused Ben to freeze, maybe it was the word cell or maybe it was an accumulation of everything that happened. He was eventually pulled up and dragged along. He found his balance and followed them through a security door into the holding cell section. He was relieved to see there was no one else there. He was shoved inside and he jumped when the door clicked in place. He put his hands up so the cuffs could be removed. He rubbed his wrists and stepped back. He crossed his arms over his chest waiting for the sheriff to fill him in.

The sheriff walked up to the bars. He was having fun with this boy but now he was real serious. "Your little girlfriend was arrested for attempted manslaughter." He took a step back. "What do you think of her now?"

Ben sat down on the bench as his world spun in circles. He needed a moment to think. But then he remembered what she told him earlier that day. "Her ex was abusing her." He stood back up taking a stand for her.

Sheriff Jones stepped closer to Ben taking his stand. "Now there's no proof of that. She never reported any abuse. Justin is an upstanding citizen of this fine community and a member of our church. Never misses a Sunday mass. The kind of man that helps old ladies cross the street and makes sure he calls his mamma every week." He paused and stepped even closer to the bars. "Now I can't say the same for Emmaline. I don't know what happened in college but she quit going to church, had all sorts of crazy ideas in her head. She embarrassed herself and her father. And now she put some crazy ideas in her mother's head too. Good thing her brother still has some sense in him." He shook his head before finishing. "I, for one, was glad to see her go. Caused too much trouble around here anyway with her cases, but I won't bore you anymore. I'll see you in the morning." He laughed as he walked away.

Ben sat back down not amused by anything that was going on. His mind was racing. He did not want to believe what he just heard but he knew there had to be some truth to it. Just how much he had no idea. He had not pushed her to talk about her past but what he was hearing was big. She should have told him. He felt his anger rising again. How could Emma not mention any of this? If she did not want to be judged she should have been truthful right from the beginning.

And now he was stuck in hell with no place to go, a lot of crap running through his mind. Maybe it would have been better to have some company. Maybe not, he thought; too many bad stories. It was going to be a long night. Ben leaned his head against the concrete wall and closed his eyes trying to pretend he was anywhere other than in a jail cell.

Emma wanted to cry but she had no emotions left. She felt bad for Ben. She could not imagine what he was thinking. She was sure the sheriff was telling him a bunch of lies or at least twisting the truth, confusing Ben even more. He must hate her and she dragged him into all this with very little warning. She should have known better. She should have forced her mother to leave. But she also understood her mother's need for the few things she wanted. Emma had taken very little with her and she was sure her father had gotten rid of the rest. Her mother, on the other hand, had a much longer history in the house and it was definitely harder for her. She had no idea if he would even talk to her in the morning but they came together and they would at least leave together. She put her knees up to her chest and closed her eyes in attempt to get any sleep she could.

Emma was woken up by the sound of the bars unlocking. Her head was pounding, her mouth was dry and her stomach was growling. Sleep came in spurts, interrupted by bad dreams and flashes from her old life with Justin. She knew Ben was a good man. Though she probably screwed up too much already. She would not blame him if he left her for good his time. For now she had to focus on getting her mother and getting out of this town. And that would definitely be for good this time.

A female deputy, different from the night before, motioned to Emma to get up. "Come on, you are free to go. You can go to the desk and pick up your personals."

She picked up her envelope noting that there was no one there from the previous night and no apologies. She could file a complaint, even sue them but it would be a waste of her energy. That would be her last trip there. She pulled out the keys to the van and waited for Ben.

Ben woke up in a similar state as Emma. He had even less sleep though. His dreams flashed between old girlfriends and Emma. It was the torment of his life right now. Torn between the simple no strings attached life and the risk of love. So far the payouts have not been worth the risk.

He still needed to get out of this situation. He had no idea what type of law Emma practiced but he was ready to call his own lawyer if needed. When the deputy came to his cell he was ready to demand to speak to a lawyer or a judge or anyone with more authority. And anyone with a bit of sanity would be a plus. So far Ben was not impressed with this town.

The opening of a door jarred him into full awareness. He stood up and stretched his aching muscles. He watched as a different deputy walked his way. He was ready to speak his demands. "I insist I speak with a lawyer or see a judge," Ben said with as much confidence as he could muster.

The deputy snarled at him. "It appears there will be no charges. Of course if I was in charge you would be staying with us much longer. However I ain't in charge so I guess you are free to go."

Ben was afraid to believe him. Emma did tell him they would be free in the morning. Looks like she was right.

"Come on boy, I ain't got all day. Your girlfriend is waiting for you."

Ben wasted no more time and followed him out. He saw Emma waiting and just as ready to leave as he was. Beyond that she was showing no expression. He did not know what he should have expected. A smile at seeing him would have been nice. His hands were clenching, his mind was turning numb. A few more hours he would be back in his apartment and it would be over.

Chapter 15

As they walked out of the police station Emma could feel the anger and confusion radiating off Ben. She was not worried about it though, she wasn't even nervous. She was over being nervous around him. After today he would still be by her side or not. There was not much she could do about it, it would be his decision. Of course in hind sight, she might have told him a little more about her past but it did not matter now. She would just have to straighten out anything the deputies told him.

They got in the van, this time Emma heading to the driver seat.

"I can't believe they let us go."

"I told you they were just messing with us."

Ben wanted to yell and scream at someone but he knew it would do no good. They obviously played by their own rules. There was no record of what happened, he was glad to let it go and stay clear of this town and go home as quickly as possible.

"We'll, let's go get your mother," Ben said going around to the passenger side.

"We will, soon."

Ben slammed his door shut not understanding why they were not going right away but he also had some personal issues that needed attention. "You have some major explaining to do."

Emma put the van in gear. "I know but I just really need food and a cup of coffee right now."

"Food?" Ben looked at ever incredulously, "we just spent the night in jail and food is all you can think about?"

"It's no big deal Ben. Besides it's still really early and I have not eaten since breakfast yesterday."

"No big deal? Maybe for you since it apparently was not your first time," he responded with sharp edge of sarcasm.

Emma held a tight grip on the steering wheel. He was right of course but it still stung to hear the words.

Ultimately she decided not to respond. He will hear it all but not until she had some sustenance in her.

Ben saw her reaction and immediately felt bad but not enough to apologize. How else was he supposed to react? He thought he was going on a ride to pick up her mother, and he ended up in jail. The only thing he had to go on was the thirty second synapses of her life. He should have ignored Allie's advice not to press too much. He always sensed that something major must have happened to cause her to relocate. He did know one thing, whatever she told him over breakfast was likely going to make or break their relationship. She was going to have to be completely truthful or he was not sure he could trust her.

They pulled into a local diner and went inside. It was a classic old diner with booths covered in vinyl; tables trimmed in fake chrome and old mini juke boxes at each table. The waitresses even wore pastel colored calf length dresses. Emma did not think it was out of nostalgia, she really thought they were just truly old uniforms.

After being seated at a booth, they quickly read the menu and the waitress took their order.

"You should eat Ben."

"I am not hungry."

"Fine, suit yourself."

The waitress was pretty quick to pour their coffee. They both took a long swig of the mediocre liquid. It was better than nothing after having been offered nothing by the not so very hospitable jailers. Not that she should have expected anything but it was not like they were real criminals.

Now that Ben had a little caffeine in him he was out of patience. He leaned forward and gave her a hardened stare. "You need to start talking Emma. And I don't want the short version, I want to hear everything."

Emma sighed as she ran her fingers though her now oily hair. He deserved to know whether or not she felt like talking about it. Her plate of pancakes came. She ordered the tall stack, she was ravenous. She poured syrup over them and took a few large bites before she started. When her hunger pains started to subside she started telling Ben what he wanted and deserved to know.

"Growing up I thought I had a reasonably normal childhood. I had a few close friends and we did all the normal things girls do. We had sleepovers and went to the mall and the movies. But it was made very clear from an early age that academics were my priority. My dad is a lawyer and he always wanted one of his offspring to be by his side."

"What about your brother?" Ben asked

"No matter how hard my dad pushed him he just could not make the grade." Emma paused to eat more of her breakfast. "You see Ben, my dad is a big fish in a small pond, he has hand in just about everything in this town. Hence why we spent the night in jail but were never charged with anything."

"Anyway, I was groomed to be a lawyer. Study hard, play very little and go to church. Those were the basic rules of my life. There were no dance classes or soccer. The only extracurricular activity I was allowed was the debate team. Oh and of course there was no dating." She paused and thought about that for a moment. "Maybe you were right, maybe it was my father's intention to convince me that no guy would be interested in me."

Ben looked at her sad eyes. "I only meant it as a joke. Most fathers go a little nuts when their daughters date."

She half smiled back at him. "I think most of the guys at school were afraid of my dad so I would not have even known if anyone was interested. No one was brave enough to try anyway."

"I would have been. Well maybe it would have been a secret relationship."

"I don't think I would have been brave enough." Emma cleared her plate and waved for more coffee.

"After high school, I went away to college. It was a whole new world for me. I was a little lost at first but like always my studies had to come first. Once I settled into my classes I started looking for other things to do. I talked my dad into letting me join the outdoor club. I figured it was just one club but I could learn how to do all sorts of things I never had. My dad was reluctant but finally agreed as long as I kept my grades up."

"So your dad still had that much influence over you even in college."

Emma shrugged, "like I said, I did not know any better. In any case, he was the one paying for my tuition."

"I can see why he felt he had some say on what you did." Ben was thinking that so far her childhood and college years seemed to be pretty normal. Most parents want to see their kids excel in school.

"That was where I met Justin," Emma continued. "We went on all the club trips together. It was hard for me at first, I felt so weak and that is when I started working out regularly. Justin never said he minded, I always made a point to go while he was in class or at the computer labs. Anyway, I learned to ski, rock climb, kayak, white water raft and survive in the woods. And I even got my motorcycle license. It had nothing to do with the club but I had a friend who was getting one so I went along. My parents did find out but once I passed the test there was nothing they could do about it."

"Those four years were really good for me. My relationship with Justin was good, or so I thought." Emma gazed into Ben's eyes with a sultry look. "At least until I had something to compare it to."

Ben softened a touch and smiled at that. "So what happened after college?"

"I went to law school and Justin got his MBA and started working in real estate development. I went to work for my father and we moved in together."

"Did you end up liking being a lawyer?"

"For the most part. But my father used me. He wanted me to do charity work and handle all the women's rights cases. Basically it just looked good for his firm.

"Back at home, I did all the things I thought I was supposed to do because that is what my mother did. I cooked, cleaned and took care of Justin's needs. It was fun for awhile; we even kept up with some of the activities we did in college. We went skiing and hiking but eventually that all faded. We were both working too hard and it became too time consuming. I tried to replace that with girl's nights out but neither Justin nor my father approved. It was unprofessional they said. I was starting to fall under Justin's control.

"The ironic thing was that I represented women in the exact same situation all day long but I did not see that it was happening to me." Emma had to stop for a moment. She had to fight back a tear. "No matter everything else that happened, the fact that I fell victim is what I hated the most."

"What about your mother and brother, did you ever try to talk to them?"

"My dad has too much of a hook in my brother's financial well-being and he is too scared to try to make it alone. My mother played the perfect wife. She volunteered with the church and school, hosted dinner parties and charity events. She did what was proper and correct as long as it made my dad look good. It was when I left for college that things started to change for her. She no longer had quite as many functions to manage. I tried to get her to join a book or sewing club but there was always an excuse why she couldn't.

"I moved back home briefly after law school and she seemed fine again. But it was not long before Justin and I got our own place and that is when that she supposedly started falling and covering bruises. I admit that even I chalked it up to clumsiness. My father would never do that. Here I was representing abused woman at his request, I did not believe he would ever lay a hand on anyone."

"When did you realize that it was him?"

"The first time Justin hit me. It was about a year ago. I carried a heavy work load and my father would not spare another lawyer for charity. I came home late one night and I was tired. I had eaten dinner at work. On my way to the shower I suggested to Justin that he throw some leftovers in the microwave. He grabbed my wrist and told me he would wait until I was done. I told him no, that I would be going to bed. He stood up and slapped my face telling me that was unacceptable."

Emma watched as Ben grew tenser. He looked like he wanted to hit something. She unfurled his hand from his coffee cup before he broke it. She placed his hand on the same place on her cheek and held it on place. She leaned her head into his soft caress. It had an instant calming effect on both of them.

"But you did not leave him then did you?"

Emma knew it was not meant to be a judgmental question. She closed her eyes and went on. "I was going to. I packed a bag and went to my parents' house. I was shocked by what had happened but even more so by what my mother had to say. 'You know men, sometimes they get a little angry. It's our job to make sure they don't get that way. Justin is a good man and should feel lucky to have him.' My father said he would take care of it. I think what he told Justin was that it was okay to keep me in line from time to time but he would have to apologize.

"Which he did, he groveled and promised to never do it again. He even took me on a weekend kayaking trip. On our tenth anniversary he asked me to marry him. I readily accepted, after all I was lucky someone liked me enough to marry me. What a joke Ben, I can't believe my parents had me so brain-washed.

"Things remained the same until the holidays came. The second time he hit me was pretty much the same as the first. I threatened to leave and he apologized. But I swore to myself if he did it again that would be the end. It was easier to wish that he wouldn't. At that point it was better than thinking of starting over. Half the women I represented left their men. The other half kept going back. I never understood it until then. It's scary facing the fall-out."

"But you did."

"Something finally clicked in my brain. It was the holiday season. There were parties to attend, dinners to host along with work and house chores. I was barely keeping up, barely staying awake. I was in the kitchen when he asked if I could bring him a beer. The only cold ones were in the garage so I told him where to find one. He got up and came into the kitchen. He asked me what was for dinner. I had no energy and told him there were leftovers and that I was going to bed. He went ballistic on me. Told me that was unacceptable and that I better not do that as his wife. It was the word wife that got me. I realized I could not be his wife. I told him if he did not start helping I was not going to be his wife. He slapped me really hard and told me I was to do as I was told. It stung really badly but I was not going to show it. I picked up a knife and told him if he touched me again I would cut his guts out and fry them for his dinner. He just laughed at me and told me to make him something to eat. I was so angry; I stood ready and told him to make it himself. He stopped and turned and looked at me with such rage. I planted my feet and tightened my grip on the knife. He came at me and slammed his fist into my jaw. It hurt but it was not enough to knock me off my feet."

"You stabbed him."

Emma finally opened her eyes nodding. Ben was trying to maintain a blank face but she could feel the tension ebb and flow through his hand. "I did but he kept coming at me. He wrapped both his hands around my neck and he started choking me. I was not as strong as I had been so I was not able to release his grip. I did manage to grab another knife and stuck that one through his stomach as well. He finally dropped to the ground. He would not shut up though; he kept screaming obscenities at me. When I caught my breath I lightly placed my foot on the knife handle and told him to shut up.

"For a brief moment I thought about leaving him there and running away. But being the lawyer that I am I knew that would make me a fugitive. So I called 911."

"And you got arrested, what about him?"

"He had two knives in him. I had some red marks. It was my word against his. There was no documented history of abuse; my parents certainly were not going to vouch for me. My mother was too scared and upset and I was ruining my father's reputation. So I went to jail for attempted manslaughter. I could have killed him if I wanted, cut his femoral artery or his jugular and let him bleed to death. I could have also posted my own bail but to me that would have been a waste of money that I knew I was going to need. Luckily Justin insisted on paying for most of the bills so I saved quite a lot of money.

"Do you know that not one person visited me? That shows how much influence my dad has on this town and that is when I decided I was going to pack up and leave. I managed to negotiate a deal that allowed me to plead guilty to assault with time already served. When I was released, I packed a few things, emptied my bank account and got in my car and drove. I stopped in Virginia. I spent a week contemplating what to do with myself. For the first time in my life I got to decide. I thought back to the few things that made me happy. That's when I set up my kayak business.

"I planned on living a single life." She finally pulled his hand away from her cheek but she still held onto it. "You kind of ruined that for me," she said jokingly.

"You know I would never hurt you."

"I know that Ben, but you have to remember that it took ten years for Justin to lay a hand on me. It was just a long slow plot to control my life." She paused and quietly added, "I really do trust you though. I can feel it in your hand."

They sat in silence contemplating the night and how they ended up in the diner and where they wanted to go. Neither one wanted to speak. They were both flawed and their relationship was flawed. Still they each had a desire to reconnect despite their fear of rejection.

The waitress brought their check and Ben grabbed it first. While Ben went to pay, Emma went to the ladies' room to run water over her face and through her hair. It wasn't a shower but it would have to do. They met back up and headed to the van. Emma walked to the driver's side but Ben stayed right behind her. Before she was able to open the door he turned her around to face him. Even though they were both grimy Ben wanted to feel Emma again, taste her and smell her sweetness.

He ran his hand through her hair and peered into her eyes trying to read her. "What do we do now?" he asked her.

Emma looked away from the piercing look. She knew what he meant but was not ready to answer his actual question. They were still stuck in this town. "We go get my mom and get out of here."

Ben stepped back crossing his arms over his chest. "I meant us."

Emma was getting impatient. She thought she knew the answer but looking at him made her a little irritated. "I don't know Ben. At first you seemed so patient but now you seem to get angry easily and you were quick to be judgmental and even quicker to jump back into your old ways."

Ben was quick to snap back, "what about you? You don't accept help, you are closed off." He stepped back towards her and looked at her hard, "then you pretend you don't know how beautiful you are yet you fall prey to anyone that shows you a bit of attention."

Emma was tired of hearing the same thing from him. "Well Ben, either you are going to get over it or you're not. I'm not the one who almost slept with someone. Even after seeing me you still brought her back to your apartment." Her voice was rising and she was starting to tremble. She thought he finally understood her but obviously he would not be able to get over the kiss. She turned and opened the door. "I'm going to get my mom. You can either get in the van or you can thumb it back to New York."

Ben balled his fists. If it had been his van he would have had no problem punching his fists though the window. She was right, he could be short tempered. It did not help he could not control his emotions around her. And he did not know how the conversation took such a wrong turn. It was not what he meant. He walked around to the passenger side and got in. "You are not going back to that house alone," he said gruffly.

Chapter 16

They rode the short drive in silence. Emma had to concentrate to keep her grip loose on the steering wheel. Her anger was still rising. And now fear was mixing in. She had no idea if her mother was still there and what she was thinking. Maybe they should have gone there first instead of the diner. But she felt she needed to be alert which she would not have been able to do on an empty stomach and after a horrible night's sleep. She pushed her feelings for Ben aside as they pulled up the driveway once again. She hoped the deputy did as she asked and let her mom know what happened. She was not sure what they would do if she was not there.

Ben walked briskly to the door with Emma trailing behind. He pounded on the door and crossed his arms. When it was not answered right away he pressed the doorbell several times. After another minute they finally heard footsteps. The door opened a crack. They expected to see a female but instead they were greeted by the barrel of a gun. Ben instinctively pushed Emma to the side out of the line of fire. And at the same time a rough hand grabbed his other arm as the door was flung open.

A man in his late twenties kept the gun pointed at them as he indicated for them to follow him inside the old house. Ben was on full alert as he entered but could not believe he was looking into another gun. He did not know what was worse, being faced with guns two days in a row or seeing Emma and Kirsten together two days in a row. The problem was this guy looked nuts which made him dangerous.

He assessed the situation. He was definitely bigger and stronger than this guy. He could overpower him given the opportunity. Without moving his head he looked around. Other than a table lamp there was not much in the way of weapons. His thoughts were interrupted when he heard Emma yell and push past him

"What the hell are you doing Justin?"

Ben grabbed Emma's arm. He did not trust this guy and did not know if he was trigger happy. He looked at the asshole that caused Emma such pain. He seemed fairly ordinary, average height with short sandy hair parted down the middle. He was wearing a sports jersey, jeans and sneakers. He had a wild look in his eyes and that made Ben nervous. He held on to Emma even though she was struggling to get away. "Take it easy Emma, you don't want to provoke him," Ben said quietly in her ear.

Emma was beyond angry, but she knew Ben was right. Justin tried to kill her once, he would do it again. She took a step back and tried to calm herself. "Where is my mother?" she growled at her ex.

"She is safe and secure in the kitchen." He waved the gun in that direction, "as a matter of fact why don't we all join her."

Ben and Emma backed into the kitchen. As soon as Emma saw her mother she jumped to her side. Her mother was tied to a chair. Her hair was a mess and she had black streaks running down her face, Savannah was sitting at her feet, ears pricked and quietly growling at the gunman.

She pushed her hair away. "Are you okay?"

She nodded and with a trembling voice said, "I'm sorry, I should not have sent you back to the house last night."

"It's not your fault." Emma started to untie the knots when she caught a motion in the corner of her eye.

"Back off," Justin yelled as he stepped closer waving his gun wildly in the air.

Ben watched Emma slowly stand up. His blood was pumping and his mind was racing. He needed to buy them some time. "What do you plan on doing with Grace?"

"I am sending her back home, of course."

Emma jumped in, "why didn't my father come get her himself?"

"When I found out you were in town, I made sure your father got good and drunk last night. He's probably still passed out. I promised him I would deliver your mother back to him unharmed. A little tortured maybe but unharmed," he added with a creepy grin.

Emma balled her fists. Savannah sensed her anger and stood up and growled louder.

"You better keep that bitch under control," Justin said taking a slight step backwards.

Emma looked at her dog and then at Justin. "How were you even able to tie her up?" She knew Savannah would have protected her mother all night.

"Even old dogs sleep. She did hear me though and almost got me. She doesn't move quite as fast as she used to, does she?"

Savannah seemed to understand and she was offended. She lashed out a few harsh barks.

Emma laughed at him; she knew he was afraid of dogs. "You're such a coward. You could have just shot her."

That clearly made Justin angry. He started yelling like the crazed man he was. "I did not want any unwanted attention while I was waiting for you and I am not playing games. You two sit on the floor. After I tie you up there's going to be an accidental fire and there won't be anything left of you or your dog."

Ben and Emma knew they had to do something at that instance. Emma grabbed Ben's hand and gave it a little squeeze while she nudged Savannah with her foot. She trusted them both to keep her and her mother safe.

She knelt down next to her mother so that Justin's focus was on her, "the only thing that is going to happen is that Ben, my mother, and my dog and I are all walking out of here. I don't give a shit what you do. We are walking away." She steadied her hands and started working on the knots.

"I told you to back off," Justin yelled.

The next few seconds were a blur in slow motion. Justin clicked the safety of the gun off. Savannah jumped at him as Ben rushed towards him as well. A shot was fired but before a second one went off Savannah clamped her strong jaw down on Justin's arm causing the gun to go flying across the floor. With the gun out of reach Savannah fell to the ground and Ben jumped in knocking Justin to the ground. He straddled him and forced his arms behind him. Justin tried to buck but Ben yanked him to his feet and clamped down harder on his arms.

Emma saw the gun go flying and made a quick grab for it, she knew Justin got a shot off and her heart sank when she turned around. Savannah was lying in a heap on the floor; there was a trickle of blood coming from her chest. She rushed over to her and laid a hand on her chest. There was nothing, no heartbeat, no breath. Her dog made the ultimate sacrifice for her. She leaned down and gave her one last kiss on the head.

She stood up with a tight grip on the gun. She stepped forward and pressed the barrel against Justin's forehead. "You low life scum. I should have killed you the first time. I should have slit your femoral artery and watched you bleed to death."

Justin tried to kick out but Ben threw him off balance. He clamped down on the wound on his wrist which caused him to buckle at the knees. Ben looked at Emma and saw the coldest icy glare he ever witnessed, her sanity was about to break and he needed to talk some sense into her. He did not want to see her back in jail. He calmed his own sense and said in soft tone, "Emma put the gun the down."

Emma turned her icy glare on Ben, "why the hell shouldn't I kill him? I went to jail because of him. I wasted ten years of my life on this loser and now he killed my dog. If I shoot him I'll claim self defense." She stared into Justin's eyes. She was enjoying the fact that they were now full of fear. Emma was ready to pull the trigger when she heard her mother.

"Emma honey," she said softly. Emma looked back at her. "He's not worth it. You may be able to walk away but you will have to live with it for the rest or your life. You already went though enough. Please honey, put the gun down. I need you," she pleaded with her daughter. "I can't get through this without you."

Emma looked from her mother to her ex and to Ben. Tears started rolling down her cheeks. Her hands started trembling again. Her mother was right. And she could not abandon her now. She looked at Justin for the final time. "You don't deserve to live. You're a piece of shit but she's right, you are not worth it. We are walking away. I don't care what you tell my father but if either one of you send anyone after us I will hunt you down. Understand?"

Justin glared at Emma, "you better not come back to this town."

"No problem." Emma freed her mother and Ben sat Justin down in the chair and tied his legs and feet, Emma was sure her father would eventually come by when her mother did not show up back home. He hoped her father found Justin before Anne came home but there was nothing she could do about that.

Emma gave her mother a long awaited hug. Ben found a blanket in which to wrap Savannah. Emma was grateful for the gesture. With sad eyes she said, "I know where we can take her to be cremated."

Ben nodded and picked her up and they all left the house together.

Chapter 17

Ben drove them back to the city. After many tears mother and daughter fell fast asleep in the back. Ben was not physically showing it but he was crying inside. He was crying for the torment these two beautiful women had endured. Crying for almost losing the woman he loved, crying for being an idiot and letting his jealousy and anger get to him. And crying for the loss of a beautiful dog that was the ultimate hero.

Without making any stops they made it back to the city in swift time. He had already talked to Allie and filled her in. Alex was staying with Katie and Allie agreed to let Grace stay with her. Ben had her book another room for Emma. She could choose to be alone but he was hoping she would let him stay with her.

Once they were in their rooms, Ben did what he had done once before for Emma. He drew hot baths for the weary ladies. He poured in lavender scented bubbles and bought water and chocolates. Once Emma and her mother were in their tubs Ben sat down with Allie and went into detail with what went down.

"You guys are lucky to be alive," Allie said when he was finished. "I can't believe Justin did that. I didn't really know him but I did not think he was capable."

Ben considered for a moment, "I think that is why we are alive. Deep down he is a coward and I think Emma knew that. She was brave to the point of stupidity but we were at a standstill. She gave me the go ahead to take him down. Fortunately and unfortunately Savannah got to him first and she paid the price."

Allie bit her lip fighting back tears. "She was a good dog. It was like she knew she was meant to be with Emma."

The two sat in silence for a few minutes. "You know Jason had a star named after Molly's sister. Maybe you could do the same for Savannah."

"Yeah, I think she would like that."

Allie looked hard at Ben, "so what are you going to do now?"

"Take you guys home, make sure Emma is okay and that no one bothers her." He sat back with his arms crossed. There would be no arguing that he was taking them all home.

Allie looked at him with squinted eyes, "I think you know want I mean."

Ben rubbed his hands through his hair. He knew what she meant and he knew what he wanted. He just was not sure how to make it happen. "I love her, Allie," he said softly.

"So tell her," Allie said leaning closer to Ben.

"I think I may have screwed up too much." He remembered how she pointed out his flaws. She was right. He was jealous and short tempered. He did not mean to be, his emotions were all over the place. He was always able to keep them under control until he met Emma.

"Ben, you both screwed up. But it does not mean you should give up on each other. Emma needs a good solid man who will treat her well. And you are it."

"I need her too," Ben said before Allie could. Ben needed her softness, her courage, her sense of adventure and her humor.

Grace came out of the bathroom wrapped in a soft terry robe. She sat down with Allie and Ben. Her eyes were still a bit puffy but she looked better. "I don't know how to thank you. Both of you. Ben for everything and Allie for being Emma's friend when I couldn't."

Ben grabbed her hand and squeezed it. "Everything is going to be okay now."

She slowly nodded. "Eventually. I have a lot of making up to do with Emma. I can not believe I kept trying to talk her into going back to him. I did not stand by her side in court. I did not defend her to her father. I did so many things wrong."

Ben knew a little about that. "I did too. She loves you Grace, she will help you through this and help you with the divorce. She's incredibly strong and focused. I still can't believe she is a lawyer."

"She was very good at it. Maybe a little too good for her father's liking. It's scary though and I know she will help me. If she had the courage to start a new life then I can too. I just have to figure out what to do with myself." She smiled at the hope of a new life. A life that she controlled. She squeezed Ben's hand in return. "Go to Emma now and help her. You two need each other right now."

"If she will let me," Ben said with a sigh.

"Don't give her a choice," Grace said with a smile.

There was something to a mother's intuition Ben would never understand but he was sure to take her advice. He stood up and told the ladies to order as much room service as they wanted and went back to the other room.

Emma would have preferred a shower but since the bath was already drawn she slipped in and let the bubbles dissolve the dirt and grime. She was emotionally numb from the last two days. She really did not want to spend another night in the city but understood everyone was too tired to continue the drive. Plus Alex was more than happy to spend another night with his new girlfriend.

What she needed to do was get back home and get back to work. Alex would be heading right back to school and she was sure Allie would be leaving soon as well. She had not charged her roommates much in rent but now she would have to carry the full mortgage plus provide for her mother as well. She was happy to do that but she had to get back to work. She had no time for brooding, no time for sulking, no time for feeling sorry for herself and certainly no time for heartbreak. She knew she screwed up too many things with Ben. He had been great the last two days. She did not know what would have happened without him. But he still seemed stuck on her faults.

She did not want to stare at the ceiling contemplating the what ifs so she scrubbed her hair and body and wrapped herself in the plush bathrobe and sat down on one of the beds. As she started flipping through the channels the door opened and she saw Ben come in. She was grateful for her own room. She would have plenty of time to catch up with her mom and she did not want to relive the experience just yet. Also the memory of Savannah still was in the other room. As far as Ben coming in, she supposed she would have little choice in that.

Ben walked in surprised to see Emma already out of the bath. He pulled a chair over to the bed and sat down. "Did you have a nice bath? I thought you would have stayed in longer."

"It was fine thanks," she told him as she kept looking at the television. There was nothing that held her interest so she stopped on the Weather Channel. There was a story on the winds in California causing problems with the wild fires. Emma glanced over at Ben, "I wonder if it is causing problems with your mother's wind chimes," she said half smiling.

As if on cue Ben's phone chimed. It just happened to be a text from his mother. He read the message. Somehow the chimes did untangle and she was so happy that things had worked out for him. He needed to trust in her chimes and to prove the point she attached a photo of the untangled strands. He held it up so Emma could see. "Actually looks like the winds helped them out."

Emma looked over but shrugged it off. She was with Ben on this one. It did not mean anything to her. She flipped the channels again and left it on the Travel Channel.

Ben looked at her with a bit of concern. "I'm not leaving you alone tonight."

"Suit yourself."

"I'm driving back with you tomorrow. I plan to spend a few days to make sure no one bothers you and make sure you and your mom are doing okay."

"We will be fine."

Ben was frustrated but he promised himself to be patient. She was closing herself completely off and he needed her to open up. "I know you will be fine. You are always fine but you don't have to get through this alone."

Emma sat up pulling her robe even tighter. She did not want to hear this, "there's nothing to get through. It's over, I just need to go home and get back to work."

"You need to take a day and let your emotions go a little. Stop holding everything inside. I don't know how you can sit here and pretend nothing happened."

Emma gave Ben a hard stare, "because it is easier. If I sat back and contemplated everything I went through the last few years I might never recover. I wasted my time with Justin. I worked too hard and never vacationed. And now I have to deal with my mom who's probably going to drive me crazy. My dog is gone, my roommates are leaving." Her voice softened a little, she bit her tongue to fight back a tear.

Ben cautiously moved over to the bed and sat facing the woman he loved. "I am here for you, please let me help you."

"Sure for now and a few days. And then what, you go back to your life and that's it?"

Ben grabbed Emma's hands. "No that's not it. I am not letting you go again. Emma I love you." He spread soft kisses across her hands as he anxiously waited for her to respond.

Emma was not sure if she heard him right, "you love me? I'm a mess Ben. I can't seem to do or say the right things. I keep screwing things up with us." Her heart was pounding. Now she truly was on the verge of tears.

Ben looked deeply into Emma's eyes, "you are not perfect. I am definitely not perfect. There are so many good things that I love about you. You are beautiful and sexy and smart. I love all of you and I will not let you go. I almost lost you today. I was so scared. I hate that it took that to see what an ass I've been. Will you give me a second chance?"

Emma started to tremble as a tear slowly slid down her cheek. She nodded as she crawled up into his lap. "You know you are pretty sexy too, and a good cook and I like taking you for rides on my bike and sneaking peeks of your muscles when we kayak."

Ben wrapped his whole body around her. He buried his head in her soft hair and ran his hands up and down her back. "I missed you so much."

Emma was losing control but she had Ben to hold her up now. The adrenaline keeping her together went away. Exhaustion finally set in and the tears started flowing. "I can't believe he shot my dog," she said between uncontrollable sobs.

Ben turned so he could lean against the headboard taking Emma with him. He pulled the blanket over her and held on tight. He knew all of her pent up emotions from the last ten years, her whole life were going to come out. And when the sobbing subsided into the soft breathing of sleep he stretched both of them out into the bed and wrapped himself down the length of her body and slipped into his own blissful sleep.

When Emma woke she was still exhausted but she was refreshed and at peace. All the hell she went though led her to this moment and right now there was no place she could think of she would rather be. She rolled over and gently woke Ben by kissing his lips. They were sweet and salty at the same time and she wanted more. She leaned up on his chest and waited for his eyes to open. And when they did she was rewarded by one Ben's beautiful smiles. "Make love to me."

And he did. He made up for lost time, lost emotions. He took his time and gave her all the attention she deserved. He cherished and worshipped her body, waking up feelings she never knew. Emma opened herself completely to him and soaked in the love. "I love you too Ben." And she meant it and she finally knew it was real.

Chapter 18

The temperatures in Virginia still had not fallen. Summer was holding on tight. The full swing of tourist season was over but Emma was still booked solid for her tours. She still had not been able to find a solid reliable assistant. Sweat was pouring off her as she loaded the last of the kayaks onto the trailer. She wished she could leave them there overnight as she was coming back the next morning. Hopefully her next interview scheduled for later that day would be a good one.

She decided to be lazy and left the trailer on the driveway instead of pushing it into the garage. No one would bother them anyway. She ran into the house throwing her keys onto the table. "Hi mom."

"Hi honey, how did it go today?"

"Good, fun group today."

"I got a nice roast beef for dinner tonight."

"Sounds good," Emma yelled back as she headed for her bedroom. She flipped on her computer and logged into her Skype account so she could talk to Ben. He had been able to make it down almost every weekend over the last few weeks. And when he could not they talked on Skype in between working. He had already told her he would only have a few minutes in the afternoon to talk and she did not want to miss it. She smiled when she saw he was already logged in waiting for her. "Hi," she said touching the screen. Of course it was not the same as feeling him in person but she still felt his being in her fingers.

"I'm sorry I am not there. I have a deadline to make."

"I understand. You know I miss you." Even though it had only been a few days it was still tough every time he left. They had not yet talked about the long distance issue. Ben knew she was not interested in moving to the city and he had not indicated he was ready to leave. Some day she would work up the nerve to ask him but she felt it was still too early.

"I know, I miss you too. Especially when I see you in your work clothes and I can't be there to tear them off."

Emma leaned into the camera revealing a taste of her cleavage. "Well I guess you need to think of that when you are deciding on your deadlines."

Ben growled at her, "You are mean."

Emma leaned back. "I'll stop."

"No, no it's okay." He decided he needed to change the subject before his body exploded from electrical surges. "So how is your mom?"

"She's doing well. My house is spotless everyday all the time. And it's a good thing my job is physical otherwise I would be getting fat from her cooking. I need to find a way to put her talents to use somewhere else. Although it's been nice having someone else do the chores for a change. Anyway, she is just scared. She has never had a real job although I have been trying to convince her that all the committees she has headed up were the same as a job."

"She will get there eventually."

"I know."

"So you have an interview today?"

"Yeah, I hope it works out, this guy is new to the area. I just need someone reliable at this point. His name is River; do you think that is an omen?"

"River? I think he sounds kind of crunchy," he laughed. "He'd better not be as good looking as me," Ben said looking a bit like a little boy.

"Not even possible," she smiled reassuring him. Emma looked at the time. She made a pouty face, "I need to get in the shower."

"You are being mean again."

"I can point the camera at me and keep the curtain open," she said as she flung off her shirt.

Ben was breathing hard, he wanted to say yes but he was on a time schedule as well. He pretended to bang his head on the counter. "No, go ahead. But I will hold you to a raincheck on that."

"Love you," she said. She flung off her sports bra just before she turned the power off. She knew it would torment him but knew he loved it as well.

Thirty minutes later she pulled up in front of the Starbucks on her motorcycle. It was a beautiful day for a ride and after the interview she planned on a ride down to the beach. She pulled her laptop out of her saddle bags, bought a cold drink and settled down on the outside patio furniture. She planned to do a little work on her website while she waited for her interviewee to arrive. She was not sure what he looked like but she told him where she could be found. While she arrived a little early she really hoped he would be on time. That was definitely one of her job requirements. She ran a punctual business and she knew her clients appreciated it.

She finished uploading her images from the morning and answered her messages. It was a few minutes past the scheduled meeting. She started to feel deflated but she was not going to give up hope just yet. She turned her head when she heard the yips of a puppy. She was still missing Savannah but was not quite ready to go to the shelter to find another dog. She had cried one more time when Ben gave her the framed certificate with the star named after her dog.

The squeaky barks were getting louder and she turned to see what kind of puppy it was. Her heart skipped a beat when she saw a Doberman puppy pulling on a leash. Her ears were flopping and tongue swinging. She was so cute. Maybe soon she would find another special dog. She turned back to her work but when the puppy was at her feet she had to reach down and pet her. Emma looked up to see who was on the other end of the leash. When she saw who it was her heart skipped several beats. Ben was standing there with the goofiest smile on his face.

So far his timing had worked as well. He had come across the Chesapeake Bay Bridge and was able to stop just in time to set up his computer to log into Skype. He knew he had just enough time to get across town to meet her at his appointed time. He stuck out his hand to shake hers, "Hi, I'm River; I'm here to interview as your assistant."

Emma was still in shock and she did not know how to respond.

"You are still hiring, right?"

Emma finally found her voice, "of course. River?" She asked wondering if he made that up.

"My full name is Riverbend."

"Seriously?" Emma asked trying to suppress a laugh.

"It's where was I was conceived. You are only the third person to know so no giving away my secret Emmaline Caroline."

"My lips are sealed," she said smiling

"Back to my job interview, I'm new in town and I need a job," he said sitting down across from her.

"New in town? You live in New York."

"Not anymore." This was the tricky part. They had never mentioned where their relationship was going. He was not sure if she was ready for the next step. He knew he was and if she was not he would be apartment hunting and he would be okay with that as long she did not totally turn him away.

"What about your job? And your apartment?"

"I finished my last job and was able to make a quick sale on my place. So now it's just me, the dog and the truck with all my belongings. So now I'm homeless and jobless."

She reached down and picked up the puppy putting her on her lap. "Well then, what makes you think you are qualified to be my assistant?"

"I'm strong, I'm personable and I am willing to do whatever you tell me." He leaned towards her giving her a sinful smile.

"Anything huh?" She looked down at her computer pretending to contemplate her decision. "The salary is not very good," which was absolutely true. "But I might be able to throw in room and board in exchange for some extra work around the house." She lifted up the puppy letting her lick her face. "What do you think, should we hire him? You're a beautiful little girl. You can live with me. Did you name her?"

"No, I wanted you to pick."

"Well I think I will give it a few days. So do you really have all your belongings here?"

"Come on I want to show you something." Emma packed up her computer and picked up her puppy and followed Ben around the corner. Sure enough there was a U-Haul truck sitting in the back parking lot. "I'll follow you back to the house then I want you to take a ride with me."

Emma kissed her new puppy and placed in her in the cab. She started scratching at the window. She could not imagine what else Ben had planned. The day was already perfect. She was ecstatic over having Ben by her side every day.

Ben followed her back to her house and he backed the truck into the driveway. She wondered what he brought with him. His furniture was far nicer than the used pieces she had picked up. Plus with Allie and Alex having moved out she did have some empty rooms. They switched to Emma's van. She would have preferred to take the motorcycle but she wanted to see more of her new puppy.

Ben was more than happy to drive. He already had memorized the route to his destination. This was his final surprise. He took them down into the country and just before he made the final turn he asked her to close her eyes. He stopped at the end of a gravel drive and helped her out of the van throwing his backpack over his shoulder.

They walked a small distance with Ben holding her arm so she could keep her eyes closed. Emma knew she was standing on sand based on the ways her shoes were sinking into the ground. Ben moved his hand away and Emma opened her eyes. She was standing on a small beach overlooking the bay. There was an abandoned restaurant next to the beach and further over was a dilapidated marina. She knew this spot well; she had kayaked by it on several occasions.

"What do you think?" Ben asked her.

"It's beautiful." But she was confused as to why he had brought her there.

"It's all ours. It's my new project."

Emma's eyes widened. The already perfect day just got amazing.

"First I'm going to renovate the restaurant and get it up and running. Then imagine a bed and breakfast back there with landscaping all around and gardens out back. We will bring the marina back to life and we can have boats come in for the night or the weekend. What do you think?"

"It sounds incredible, but you know if I hire you your job with me will have to come first." She was half teasing. "But as soon as you get this place up and running I can launch right off the beach." She was getting really excited now. "Oh and my mother will be perfect to run the bed and breakfast."

"So are you with me on this?"

She turned and gave Ben a huge hug and kissed him deeply and passionately. "Now I will never have to say goodbye to you again."

Ben reached into his bag bringing out the gift his mother had sent him. It was the crazy wind chimes declaring their love. They both laughed as he held them above their heads like mistletoe and then returned Emma's kiss.

About the Author

I have been an avid reader all of my life and enjoy a variety of genres including romance, action, historical novels and anything Star Wars related. Creating stories and characters has been a new and exciting adventure for me. I love bringing my characters to life in settings I am familiar with. The goal of my books is to make people laugh, smile, maybe cry a little and just overall be entertaining.

I hope you enjoyed this book and if you have not already please consider reading my first book Julie's Star. You can contact me at lesleyespositoauthor@gmail.com

You can also follow my blog at lesleyesposito.blogspot.com

When I am not writing I am a Licensed Veterinary Technician, mother of two daughters and a wife. I also live with two dogs, a cat, a rabbit, a bunch of fish and keep a horse not too far from home. I also enjoy Scrapbooking and photography and volunteering as the treasurer of the Crescent Bay Pony Club. My other passion is dancing, I take tap and jazz with an amazing group of adults. Once a year I can be seen dancing on stage in characters such as Catwoman, Miss Argentina, Modern Millie, Morticia Adams and Ginger Rogers.